The Place at the Edge of the Earth

The Place at the Edge of the Earth

Bebe Faas Rice

Clarion Books / New York

Clarion Books
a Houghton Mifflin Company imprint
215 Park Avenue South, New York, NY 10003

The text was set in 12.5-point Eldorado.

www.houghtonmifflinbooks.com

Printed in the U.S.A.

Library of Congress Cataloging-in-Publication Data

Rice, Bebe Faas.
The place at the edge of the earth / by Bebe Faas Rice.
p. cm.
Summary: At first unhappy with a new stepfather and a new school on a military base that was once an off-reservation boarding school for Indian children, thirteen-year-old Jenny finds herself changing as she makes two new friends, one the son of the base commander and the other the ghost of Jonah Flying Cloud, who died there in 1880.
ISBN 0-618-15978-9
[1. Ghosts—Fiction. 2. Teton Indians—Fiction. 3. Indians of North America—Great Plains—Fiction. 4. Schools—Fiction. 5. Stepfathers—Fiction.] I. Title.
PZ7.R3615 Pl 2002
[Fic]—dc21 2002007405

QUM 10 9 8 7 6 5 4 3 2 1

Jacket photo (front, left) used by permission of The Cumberland County Historical Society, Carlisle, Pennsylvania.

To my dear friend Jill. Without her support and encouragement I could not have written this book.

1

Jonah Flying Cloud

There are no eagles here, in this place at the edge of the earth. . . .

The morning I left the land of my people, the Lakota—those whom the white men call "Sioux"—my father pointed to the sky and said, "See the eagle? He is sacred to us because his wings carry him to heaven, yet he chooses to live on earth, to teach us to be strong and free."

All around us, children were crying. Parents were wailing. Some were singing death chants.

"Why should we send our children to the white man's school?" they cried. "They say we must give them our children. What will they do to them?"

My father's face was stern. He was their chief, so when he held up his hand for silence, they stopped their sounds of grief and listened to him.

"The white man is stronger than we are," he told them.

"Our children must learn his ways, so they, too, can become stronger."

"His ways!" called out an old warrior named Thunder Hawk. He spat on the ground to show his scorn. "White people are thieves and liars. Do we want our children to learn such things from them at their school? The children will be far away. They will not have their fathers and grandfathers to counsel them."

"*Hau*. Yes," the people agreed, putting their arms around their children and drawing them closer.

"No, listen to me," my father said. "We have lost our lands to the white men because we believed their promises. We have set our marks, our sacred pledges, on their papers. But we could not read their words, so we did not know that these papers betrayed us. That is why our children must learn to speak and read the white man's language. Only then can we protect ourselves and our lands. The white men are coming. And they are many, as many as blades of summer grass. We must know their words so they can no longer cheat us with promises and papers."

The people were silent. Finally, an old grandmother named Spotted Pony spoke up: "Our chief is wise. If this is how it must be, so let it be."

The others nodded and said, "Yes. So let it be."

We were taken to the river and put aboard a boat with a big wheel at one end. I did not cry when I parted from my father and mother. I did not wish to dishonor them by a show of cowardice. I was the son of a chief, and chiefs' sons do not cry. But it was a sad parting, and I was much afraid.

The boat was big and noisy with the wheel turning and splashing. We children were put in a room below, in the belly of the boat. It was growing dark, but none of us were able to sleep. Many cried because already they missed their people.

One of the bigger boys, knowing I was the chief's son, took me aside and said, "Your father was wrong. The white men do not wish to teach us at that school. They are planning to kill us."

"Why do you think that?" I asked.

He sneered. "Why else? They want to see us dead before we grow big enough to kill them."

"My father would know of this, if what you say is true," I said, narrowing my eyes at him. "Besides, why did you not try to escape if you fear death at their hands?"

The boy, Swift Running River, tossed his head proudly. "I do not fear death. My father died bravely fighting Custer Long Hair. All the great battles are over now. Our people have smoked the pipe of peace and made their marks on the white man's paper. This is my only chance to die like a warrior."

I shrugged and turned away. I did not believe him. Swift Running River was known in my village as a boy who talked boldly but foolishly. That was why he had been given that name. His tongue, it was said, ran as swiftly as a river.

The next morning we were taken off the boat, put in wagons, and driven to a strange place where a long line of narrow cabins, painted dark yellow, stood end to end. Inside each cabin were rows of high-backed seats. In the wall beside every seat was a large glass window. So many windows! I had never before seen such a thing.

The white man who was traveling with us spoke our language. He told us to sit down, so we did. I was in the first cabin. Our group had been separated, with girls in some of the cabins and boys in the others. I was sorry to see that Swift Running River was in mine. I did not like him. I had never liked him.

Then, suddenly, the little cabin began to move.

The younger children screamed. Some hid beneath their blankets. I clutched the arm of my seat tightly, so I would not be flung out upon the floor.

The interpreter stood up and shouted, "Quiet, everyone! There is nothing to be afraid of. This is what the white men call a "railway train." It has iron wheels and it moves on long pieces of metal that stretch out across the land. It will take you safely to the white man's school."

Soon we all became accustomed to the rattle and movement of the train, although the sight of the countryside flashing by frightened us and made us dizzy.

We traveled all day and into the night. When we were hungry, we ate the food our families had given us for the journey, jerky and pemmican—little cakes of pounded venison mixed with fat and berries.

Ahead of us the moon—a bright, full moon—shone down on the little moving cabins that were taking us farther and farther from home. I thought of my father's tipi, and blinked back tears. My parents and grandparents would now be lying down on their beds of soft hides and furs. How I longed to be with them.

Swift Running River moved into the empty seat beside me. "I see now how the white men plan to kill us," he said, leaning forward and speaking to me in a low voice. "They are taking us to the edge of the earth."

"What do you mean?" I asked.

"Everyone knows the earth is flat," he said. "We will ride the iron pathway to the edge of the earth, and then we will all fall off."

"Why do you come to me and say these things, Swift Running River? Is it because I am younger than you, and a chief's son, and you think you can count coup by frightening me?"

"It is the truth," Swift Running River said staunchly, but he did not look me full in the eyes. "The other boys think it is so."

I turned and looked back at the other boys. They were talking quietly.

"I see no sign of fear in their faces," I said. "Nor do I see them preparing for death by painting their faces and putting feathers in their hair. Shall I ask them why they are not afraid of falling off the edge of the earth?"

Swift Running River stood up quickly. "No—no, do not mention this to them," he said.

I tried to speak with my father's strong voice. "We are going into the white man's country. We will be among enemies. We should be friends, Swift Running River, and give each other courage. That is the way of our people."

"What you say is true," Swift Running River said slowly. His face turned red with shame. "I *have* tried to frighten you. I envied you your father, since mine is dead, and so I spoke to you unworthily and with a mean spirit."

Before he went back to his friends he said, "But the earth *is* flat. Our elders teach us that. And if we travel long enough toward the sun, we *could* drop off the edge."

I was to find out later, at the Indian school, that white people believe the earth is round and that it turns and spins.

How can that be? Why are we not dizzy and falling off the ground? We are not bats, that we can cling to a perch with our toes and hang upside down.

If anyone believes the earth is flat, it should be white people. They live in a world of flatness and edges. The buildings at the Indian school were like boxes. The tables upon which we ate were arranged in long lines. Our beds were in straight rows.

On the other hand, the world of my people was round. The tipis. The lodges. The sun, the moon, the sacred circle—the symbol that all things are one and must remain forever joined.

I asked one of the teachers this question: Why do my people live round, but see the earth as flat, while the white man lives flat, yet sees the earth as round?

She could not answer. Perhaps it was because I asked the question in my poor English. When, in my eagerness for an answer, I asked it again—this time, without thinking, in the language of the Lakota—she grew very angry because I had broken the biggest, most important rule of the school. We were to speak only in English, not in our native tongues. She beat me with a leather strap and made me wash my mouth out with lye soap.

I did not ask this teacher another question. Never again.

One of the first things they did to us at the Indian school was cut our hair. They said it would make us cleaner, so that we would not have lice on our heads, but one of the interpreters, a half-breed, told us, "The white men do this to set their mark upon you, so that you will look like them."

To my people, cutting the hair is a sign of mourning. We

do it only when someone has died. The hair is the seat of the soul. The mark of a warrior, or of a good woman, is long, thick hair, shiny as a crow's wing, that hangs down below the waist.

We put our arms over our heads and begged them not to do this terrible thing to us, but they would not listen. I tried to escape the hair-cutting men by hiding under my bed, but they dragged me out and tied me to a chair.

By the end of the day, we were all cruelly shorn. When I ran my hand over my head, I felt only a short stubble beneath my fingers.

I wept with shame.

That night when we were supposed to be in our beds, both girls and boys went out to the great field that lay beyond our sleeping houses and sang death chants to show our grief. It was a high, shrill sound that pierced the heart.

Candles appeared at the windows of our teachers, yet none came out to punish us. It was very strange, since they always were ready to punish.

Maybe it was because we sounded like ghosts, and they were afraid. Or maybe it was because they knew this wailing marked our death as Indians.

And it did. The next day they took away our Indian clothing, just as they had our hair. My grandmother had given me a fine blanket with blue stripes. It was beautiful and soft and a comfort to me. I never saw it again.

We were made to wear stiff shoes that squeaked and hurt our feet. Oh, the pain of those shoes! They did not bend when we walked, and they rubbed great sores on our feet—sores that bled and made us sick and feverish and unable to walk.

They also gave us red underwear, long and tight, that scratched and burned like the bites of a thousand fleas. And, over that, thick woolen uniforms that we were forced to wear, even in the heat of summer.

The bottom part of my clothing, the trousers, had what the white man called "buttons." At first, I could not remember if the buttons went in the front or the back. We were told they went in the front, and even then I and my new friends had trouble pushing the buttons through the small holes. I wet myself several times before I became skilled at using those buttons.

We were also told we could void our bodily wastes only by sitting on a "toilet," a board with a hole in it, in what they called the "outhouse." At first, my heart pounded with fear whenever I sat upon that rough board. I was afraid an evil spirit would seize me from below, and pull me down, down, into the stinking pit. I could barely do what I needed to do, so great was my terror.

Once I wet my bed at night, because I feared going out into the darkness to sit on that demon board, and I was made to carry my straw-filled mattress on my back as a mark of shame all the next day.

They gave us new names, too, taken from something called the "Good Book."

My new name was Jonah. They told me Jonah was a man who had been swallowed by a big fish. "Please do not give me this name," I begged. "It will bring bad luck."

"Nothing from the Good Book can bring bad luck," they said, so I became Jonah Flying Cloud—my Good Book name joined to my father's name.

We lived by the sounds of bells and bugles. The white

people cut their days into little pieces, and bells and bugle calls marked those pieces.

We marched to meals. We marched to our classrooms. And when we were not studying in school, we were working for the white man. We—the sons and daughters of great warriors and mighty hunters—were made to work in his fields and in his barns, shoveling horse dung and squeezing the leathery teats of milk cows.

The interpreters left the school soon after that, and we had to learn quickly to speak English in order to survive. To keep us from speaking to each other in our native tongues, they mixed us with children of other tribes, putting us in sleeping rooms with Apaches, Navajos, and Iroquois. In this way, we had no common language and had to speak to each other in English if we were to speak at all.

I hated the food. It was soft and mushy and had no taste—the sort of thing the women of my village chewed up and spat out to feed to the old people who had no teeth. Very seldom were we given meat, and when we were it was from something called a "pig," a strange grunting animal that resembled a dog with hooves. How I hungered for a good piece of buffalo hump or a bit of liver.

They allowed us no rest. On Sunday, the seventh day of the white man's week, we were marched to their church, where we sat most of the day, listening to a man speak on and on about the white man's god. If we fell asleep, we were rapped sharply on the head by our teachers.

I did not understand the white man's religion. His god sounded to me like our Indian spirit, Wakan Tanka, the Great Holy Mystery, the Spirit of the Universe. But we were told they were not the same. We were not to worship

Wakan Tanka, they said, because it was a heathen practice, and we would burn forever in a fiery pit if we did not accept the white man's god.

This was the hardest thing of all for me to lose—the great, loving spirit, Wakan Tanka, and the beliefs of my fathers.

So in the Moon of Popping Trees, the last month of the white man's year, I realized I was not being taught to read and write in order to protect my people, as my father had wished. Instead, I was being turned into an imitation white man. I'd been robbed of my hair, my clothes, my language, my freedom, my happiness. But most of all, I had been robbed of the most sacred part of me—my spirit, my Indian spirit, that which made me who and what I was.

Others were unhappy, too. Some tried to run away. They were brought back, whipped, and thrown into the guard-house, with its four small, dark cells. They were left there, alone and in the darkness, until they confessed to their "wrongdoing" and were released.

Some escaped by dying. The white man's diseases were everywhere. They sickened and died of measles, mumps, and whooping cough. Some became ill with a plague called "tuberculosis." Some died of homesickness, turning their faces to the wall and wasting away.

I died in the month the white men call January.

Their old year had ended, and so had my life. I could no longer eat. The tea made me vomit, and the food stuck in my throat. Nor was I able to swallow the white man's bitter medicine. I spat it out. They scolded me for doing that, but I could not get it down.

I lay in my bed in the Place of Sickness, that which was

called the "infirmary," looking out the window, longing to see an eagle, swift and strong, beating his wings in an upward flight.

I saw no eagle. There are no eagles in this place at the edge of the earth.

I died, thinking my spirit would travel over the milky pathway of stars to Wanagi Yata, the place above the clouds, where the souls of my people gather.

I was wrong. I am trapped here, alone in this dark half-world between two worlds—alone and longing with a sick heart to join my people in the land above the clouds, where the eagles fly.

2

Jenny Muldoon

Until I was nine years old, I thought I'd killed my father.

We were living in a small logging town in California when he died. Dad ran a grocery store, but he was also a volunteer fireman, like most of the other men in Cedar City. Forest fires were always a threat, especially in the summer.

The August I turned five, a brushfire blazed out of control in the forest. You could hear the wailing of the fire station siren all over town. Dad and the other volunteers closed their stores and offices and rushed off to fight the fire.

Everything seemed to be going well, but just when the firefighters thought they had the flames safely put down, a sudden, strong wind arose, whipping and feeding the fire, driving it back toward them.

Dad and two others were trapped on a hillside, facing the rapidly oncoming wall of flames. The men turned and ran desperately toward the small stream that zigzagged through the valley, but the fire was faster. It overtook them, ran over them, and set them ablaze. Then it leapfrogged the stream and rampaged on, crackling, smoking, and devouring everything in its path.

All three died. It took Dad longer, though, than it did the others.

He was in a hospital bed when I last saw him. Mom led me into his room. "Daddy's . . . sick, Jenny," she whispered. "He wanted to see you. Go over and tell him you love him. Daddy needs to hear you say that. It will make him feel better."

Mom was crying. Her eyes were streaming and she kept wiping her nose with a wadded-up tissue. I'd never seen her cry like that.

I drew back and clung to her. "No," I argued. "That's not Daddy! He doesn't look like my daddy."

The man on the bed was wrapped in white bandages that smelled of strong medicine. Even his face was bandaged. Tubes ran into him from little bottles on poles. I saw a lot of wires, too, connecting him to what looked like small TV screens that kept beeping and flashing.

"Please, Jenny," Mom said, giving me a gentle push. I could feel her hands trembling on my shoulders. "Go to Daddy. Tell him you love him."

The man on the bed turned his head slightly and looked at me. I saw his eyes through the holes cut in the bandages. Yes—Mom was right. It was Daddy. Nobody had eyes like his. I called them "root beer eyes," because they were so dark brown and sparkly. It was our little joke.

"Oh, Daddy," I said, running over to the bed. "What did

they do to you? Why did they wrap you up in all that white stuff?"

Dad said something, but I couldn't hear what it was, his voice was so low and weak. He said it again, slowly, but this time a little louder.

"Jenny . . . kissed . . . me."

It was the beginning of a poem, a poem about a girl named Jenny. I knew that poem.

I waited for him to continue, but instead he stopped and made a soft, choking sound. Then his eyes filled and tears spilled out onto the bandages, leaving round, wet patches on the white gauze.

"Go on, Daddy. Say the rest," I urged, wondering what was wrong with his eyes to make them water like that.

"Please, Jenny, no," Mom said. "Daddy can't talk right now."

"But I want to hear our poem," I protested. "Come on, Daddy, I'll help you: 'Jenny kissed me when we met . . . jumping from the chair she sat in. . . .' "

The "Jenny Kissed Me" poem was Dad's and my special poem. He recited it to me all the time. It was about a man who says that although he is old and sad and poor, when Jenny jumped up from the chair she sat in and kissed him, it made him feel happy and young again.

Dad always said that's how he felt when he came home from work and I ran over and kissed him. Sometimes, just for fun, he called me Jenny-Kissed-Me, instead of plain old Jenny.

"Say the rest of it, Daddy," I repeated. I loved that poem. I thought it had been written just for me, since the girl's name was Jenny.

"Jenny," Dad said, and then he said something else, but I couldn't make out what it was.

"What? What did you say, Daddy? Wait, I'll come closer!"

Before Mom could stop me, I grabbed hold of the rail that separated Dad and me, put my foot on the metal bedframe, and pulled myself up. The whole bed shook when I yanked on that rail.

"Jenny!" Mom cried in alarm.

Dad made a sound I've never been able to forget—a sharp, painful gasp, ending in a wet rattle.

The sound frightened me. I started to cry, and Mom hurried me from the room.

My father died that night.

Nobody said I'd killed my father by climbing up on his hospital bed, but I was sure I had. For the next four years, I was convinced Dad would still be alive if I hadn't jounced him like that.

I didn't talk about it to Mom. I figured she knew I'd caused his death, and I didn't want to hear her say so. It was bad enough me thinking it without her agreeing.

Dad didn't leave us much in the way of insurance money. Once the bills started piling up, Mom realized she had to get a job. And soon.

We left Cedar City and our nice house with its big backyard. "We can't afford the rent, and there aren't many jobs in a town this size," Mom said, adding, "not that I'm qualified to do much of anything."

She eyed me sadly. "I married too young, Jenny. I should have gone to college or business school first. Now here I am with no education and no work experience. It's not fair to you."

After that, we lived in a series of cheap apartments while Mom went from one low-paying job to another, working by day, going to school at night, trying to carve a foothold for herself in some sort of career.

I didn't complain, though. I figured everything was my fault: the ratty apartments; Mom coming home white-lipped tired every night; the bored, uncaring baby-sitters who were my only companions. None of this would be happening if Daddy hadn't died. The guilt for that was always there, gnawing away on my insides.

I made no friends because I was always changing schools. Not that I even tried. I was the girl who'd killed her father. Who wanted somebody like that for a friend? I felt isolated from other kids because of my dark secret.

When I was nine and in the fourth grade, I finally worked up the nerve to talk to my mother about that day in the hospital.

"Oh, Jenny!" she cried when I'd finished, her eyes wide with horror. "No! No, of course you didn't kill your father. He was dying, and he begged to see you one more time. I didn't think I should take you in there . . . with him like that . . . but he loved you so much, and he kept asking. . . ."

She broke off and took me by my shoulders, putting her face close to mine, forcing me to look into her eyes. When she spoke again, her voice was firm. "Listen to me, darling. I'm telling you the truth, and I want you to believe me: You had nothing to do with your father's death. Nothing at all. He was in terrible pain. He only had a few more hours to live. You climbing on his bed didn't do anything to him one way or the other."

Then she wrapped her arms around me and rocked me

gently back and forth. My face rested against the curve of her neck, and I could smell the dear, familiar wildflower scent of her hair.

"Jenny," she murmured brokenly. "My poor, darling girl. Why didn't you tell me this sooner? No wonder you—"

She didn't complete the sentence. I've often wondered what she'd been about to say:

No wonder you seem so unhappy.

No wonder you are such a loner.

No wonder you're so weird.

No, Mom never would have said that last one, but it was true. I *was* weird. In my last school, I'd overheard a bunch of girls talking about me:

"Let's not invite Jenny to our sleepover," they'd said. "She's so *weird!*"

Being a loner, I read a lot. Books were my only friends. And somewhere I'd read the sentence, "As a twig is bent, so grows the tree."

I was that tree, I told myself dismally. I was nine years old, and I was bent weird—so weird that I'd lived these past four years believing something that was not true. How could I have been that dumb? Of course you can't kill somebody by jiggling their bed. Why hadn't I realized that?

I'd been like some silly little kindergartner who hears that old schoolyard rhyme, "Step on a crack and break your mother's back," and then runs home when she steps on a crack, afraid she's going to find her mother half dead on the floor.

Realizing I hadn't killed my father lifted a ton of weight off my shoulders. But, like that twig, it was too late now for me to unbend. I was a loner. I had no friends. Those girls in my class were right. I was weird, and weird was how I'd always be.

When I was twelve, though, almost thirteen, things started looking up for Mom and me.

Mom was smart, quick, and hardworking. Her night classes helped, too, and she was beginning to feel more confident about her office skills. A job as receptionist in a large real estate firm led to her being offered the position of office manager, with a substantial raise in salary.

We celebrated by moving into a really nice high-rise apartment building with a great view of the city and a swimming pool in the enclosed courtyard below. I'm not much of a swimmer, but I made plans to hang out down there and get a great tan.

And then Mom had to go and meet Major Paul Jarvis, U.S. Army.

The ladies at the real estate office started calling him "Major Dad," once he and Mom began to date regularly.

"There used to be a TV series by that name," Mom's friend Darla explained. "We all think Paul resembles the actor who played the title role."

"I wouldn't know. It was before my time," I said sullenly. Not true. Actually, I'd seen a couple of the reruns. And Paul *did* look like the Major Dad character.

Mom had dated before, but never seriously. This time it was different. Suddenly, she was seeing a lot of Paul. So was I. He was always bringing over dinner for the three of us—take-out Chinese, buckets of chicken, tacos. "Meals on wheels, bachelor style," he'd say, and Mom would act like he'd just said something terribly clever.

"He's very thoughtful," Mom said. "He knows I don't like to go out to dinner and leave you to eat by yourself."

Yes, Paul was a nice guy. Even I had to admit it. And he was good to me, including me on a lot of their dates, which is something none of Mom's previous boyfriends—if you could call them that—had ever done.

In fact, Paul actually seemed to like me, which was strange since I never went out of my way to be nice to *him*. It wasn't that I had anything against him. It's just that I felt he was an intruder. I wanted to keep things the way they'd been since Dad died—just Mom and me.

I should have seen it coming. Looking back, I see now that she'd made a number of attempts to let me know she and Paul were working up to something permanent, but I didn't pay any attention. For the last eight years it had been just the two of us, Mom and me, the dynamic duo, so I refused to accept what was going on right under my nose.

One night Mom came home wearing a diamond ring. I took one look at her hand and felt the floor drop from beneath my feet.

"That's an engagement ring, isn't it?" I gasped, staring at her in horror. "That man has given you an engagement ring! And that means you've promised to *marry* him, doesn't it?"

Mom silently removed her coat and turned to hang it on the rack beside the door.

"You have, haven't you, Mom?" I demanded, my voice rising shrilly. "How could you possibly do such a thing?"

Mom's back was to me. Her voice was muffled in the folds of her coat when she replied. "It was simple, Jenny. I merely said yes tonight when he asked me."

"This isn't funny, Mom," I snapped, hands on my hips. "We're talking serious business here."

Mom turned around slowly and faced me. "Yes, darling, I know it's serious. That's why I said no all the other times he's asked me. I wanted to make sure it was the right thing to do."

"The right thing to do?" I was practically shouting now. "What makes you think that marrying Paul is the right thing to do?"

Mom took me by the hand and led me over to the sofa. She drew me down beside her, still holding my hand.

"I guess it's right because I'm in love with Paul and I can't imagine life without him. That's what makes it right."

"Does this mean you've forgotten Daddy, and how much you used to love him?"

"No, darling. Of course not. I'll never forget your father. And I'll always love him. Surely you must realize that. But he is dead, eight years dead, and nothing will bring him back. It's time that I—and you—got on with our lives."

"And getting on with your life means marrying Paul?" I paused for effect before adding spitefully, "I never figured you were one of those women who needs a husband, just for the sake of having a man around the house, Mother."

"I think you know better than that, Jenny." Mom didn't raise her voice, but her eyes darkened, and I saw a muscle twitch in her cheek. I was surprised she didn't lose her temper and tell me off. I think, maybe, that was what I wanted her to do, so I could act abused and make her feel guilty.

"I'm marrying Paul because I love him and because he's a good, decent man who will make us both happy," she said evenly.

She shifted a little on the sofa. "Paul's never been married. He has no children. You know that. He wants very much for us to be a real family. He'd love to be a father to you, Jenny. Won't you give him a chance?"

"But you and I *are* a real family, Mom," I argued. "I don't need a fake father. You and I don't need anyone but ourselves."

At that, I saw a side of my mother I'd never seen before. She flattened me with a glance and said slowly, enunciating every word: "You'll be thirteen next week, Jenny. A teenager. In five years—five short years—you'll be going off to college. When that happens, if I try to make you stay home, to keep you here, with me, you'll tell me—and quite justifiably—that it's time I let you go, and that I should get a life for myself. I believe that's the term people use nowadays. *Get a life.*"

She took a deep breath and let it out slowly. "Well, I'm *getting* a life. A life with Paul. I hope you will give us your blessing. But with or without it, darling, Paul and I are getting married. I think you'll be happy about it, too, once you get used to the idea."

I was maid of honor at Mom and Paul's wedding. I wore a pink taffeta dress with puffed sleeves. I looked like a nerd.

Later, after the reception, as I was taking it off, I told Mom, "Don't throw this thing away. When I die, you can bury me in it. It will be absolutely perfect for my funeral."

Mom only laughed. Honestly, that woman can be really aggravating when she puts her mind to it.

I never did have a chance to hang out poolside and get my tan. Soon after the wedding, Major Dad got military orders to Fort Sayers, a miserable little army post back East, out in the middle of nowhere, so we had to pack up and move.

Fort Sayers was old, one of the oldest posts in the country. It had been many things over the years. In the late 1800s it had been a boarding school for Indian children.

I didn't know there'd ever been special boarding schools for Indian children. Not that I'd ever given it much thought.

We moved into a set of old white military quarters that looked out over the parade field. I don't know exactly how old those quarters were, but they were all attached, sort of like a row of wooden town houses, except that they all had railed porches on both the ground and second-story levels.

Paul explained that the railings had once been connected, making long upper- and lower-level verandas. This upper story, he explained, had been used as dormitories for the Indian students, while the ground floor had been broken up into classrooms. Then he went on to say—like I'd be thrilled to death to hear this—that our particular set of quarters at the end of the building had been used as the school infirmary.

"You mean, *sick* kids used to live here?" I asked.

He and Mom exchanged glances.

"Yes," he said. "This is where they used to keep the sick students."

I realized later that some of those sick Indian students might have died in our house.

But I didn't think about it at the time because I was worrying about attending the on-post school. It was going to be tough. Those kids all knew each other. They'd been stationed together, growing up. They were all army brats. They walked the walk and talked the talk, and I'd be the outsider.

Again.

As usual.

Would they like me?

Probably not.

You'd think I'd be used to being an outsider by now, but no. This time it would be even worse. I didn't know anything about the army. Already, even without meeting them, I hated those smug little army brats, all banded together against the civilian outsider. Me.

This, I thought, was it. The last straw.

This time I'd finally hit rock bottom. My life couldn't get any worse. I was alone again and miserable out here in the middle of nowhere—alone in this place, this godforsaken place at the edge of the earth.

3

Jonah Flying Cloud

There were many deaths at the school, right from the beginning. Almost immediately, students began to sicken and die, and their parents were not told of it until it was too late.

"This is not fair to our people," I said. I had been at the school only one moon at this time. It was now the Moon When the Cherries Turn Black. The white man calls it "August."

"This will not happen when we learn to read and write," I continued. "We will be able to send messages to the families then."

"It will do no good, even when we learn to write," said Isaac Red Elk, one of the mixed-bloods. Isaac already spoke the white man's language and understood, better than most, what was going on around us. "Mr. Samuel, the chief of the school, reads everything that comes in and goes out. He would tear our letters up."

"Why?" I asked. "Why would he do such a thing?"

"Because he is a Wasichu—a white man—and wishes to kill us," Swift Running River hissed. "This is his way of doing it."

Swift Running River still hung close about me, like a friend, even though he was older than I. Maybe it was because he was of my band and my village, and admired my father, the chief. Or maybe it was because he had no friends his own age. The older boys said he was a troublemaker, and avoided him.

"No, Mr. Samuel is not trying to kill us," Isaac said, shaking his head vigorously. "If we all died, there would be no school, and then where would he be? He likes being chief in this place. The reason he does not tell the parents about their sick children is because he is afraid the Indian fathers will come, bringing holy medicine men, to cure them."

He lowered his voice and glanced quickly over his shoulder to make sure we were not being overheard. We were speaking Lakota, which was strictly forbidden. "I myself heard him tell a teacher that medicine men are filthy heathens, and wicked unto death in the eyes of the Wasichu god."

"I do not believe the white man's god thinks this," Swift Running River said, his eyes flashing. "He is good and kind, like our Wakan Tanka. It is said he sent his son down from the sky to help the white men, but they killed him. They hung him from a cross until he was dead. I do not understand why the great Wasichu Father God does not destroy these terrible people."

All this was said in the beginning. By the time I died, Isaac had run away from school. Even with all his searchers and dogs, Mr. Samuel was not able to catch him and bring him back. I liked Isaac. I hoped he found his place and his people again.

As for Swift Running River . . . already his hatred of the Wasichus had set his feet on the snakepath of bitterness and violence.

In those early days I kept remembering what my father had said when I left my village: that I was here to help my people by learning as much as I could about the white man's ways. Since our chiefs could not understand the white man's language or his written word, they did not know when they were being lied to, or given pieces of paper that meant nothing.

I would learn to read and write and speak the white man's language, I vowed. I would listen and learn in order to save my people from the Wasichus, who, even then, were taking from us our beloved and sacred Paha Sapa—the Black Hills—because in those hills lay the yellow metal that drove white men crazy with the lust to possess it.

Our teachers, with their hairy faces and bodies and thick clothing that smelled of sweat, told us we were barbarians, and that we were ignorant and dirty because we were not civilized. They said that their civilization would triumph over our savagery, and that a white man's education was our only chance to step from darkness into the light.

"At this school," Mr. Samuel said, "we will lead you from your savage ways and teach you the ideas and behavior of civilized people."

Civilized and *civilization* were words we heard over and

over again every day. We listened, and as time passed, we began to fall under their spell, because we were only children and were far away from our families. And because children's memories are short, the stories our grandfathers had told us about the bravery and honor and decency of our people slowly faded from our minds.

We were shown drawings of Indians on the warpath—Indians with long knives, scalping women and children. Did we want to be like them? No. Indians were bloodthirsty savages. We wanted to be civilized, like the white man.

And so, little by little and bit by bit, we were twisted and changed and warped and remade in the white man's image.

I was the son of a Lakota chief, and the grandson of a great Lakota warrior. I was supposed to follow in their footsteps. I had a duty to grow up and lead my people. Instead, my Indian spirit was stolen from me, and I fell into a crack somewhere between the world of the white man and the world of my people.

I failed my father and my people.

That is why I did not fail Swift Running River, the moment he most needed me.

When I died they put me in a rough pine box and buried me six feet under the ground. Only then was a message sent to my father and mother, by way of the nearest Indian agency, telling them of my death.

My parents and relatives must have grieved to know that I had died alone, so far from home, without those I loved there beside me, to mourn me and prepare me for my journey on the Spirit Pathway.

The Wasichu minister said some words over my burial box before dirt was heaped upon it, and read from the Good

Book about the white man's paradise. But there were no other ceremonies. Nothing to send me on my way to Wanagi Yata, the place where the souls of my people gather after death.

Watching from behind the shadow-veil that now separated me from the land of the living, I thought of my village, and my grandfather's burial.

I remembered how he was mourned. How we wailed and sang grief songs while he was being prepared for his spirit journey. How his blood kin cut their hair and slashed their arms as a sign of their sorrow.

My grandfather's face was painted with the marks that showed his feats in war, and he was dressed in his finest garments. He had been a great warrior-leader, so he wore in death his ceremonial hair-fringed war shirt and leggings, which only a man of his status and achievement was privileged to wear. On his head was a headdress of eagle-tail feathers, each feather signifying a special war honor.

His body was then wrapped in a soft buffalo skin. Over that was a heavy rawhide robe that covered him from head to foot, and it was tied around with rawhide ropes.

The hide-wrapped bundle that was my grandfather was carried by pony drag a short distance from our village and was placed on a platform that had been erected on tall poles. My father and uncles lashed the bundle securely to the platform, so that it could not be dislodged by storms and strong winds.

There Grandfather's body would lie, not under the dirt as mine did, but under the vast dome of the sky, while his soul made its way over the archway of stars to Wanagi Yata, that beautiful land of green hills and clean, pure lakes, where every tipi had great racks of meat drying beside it, and where the spirits of my people lived together forever in peace and plenty.

Afterward my father took me aside and said, "Remember this day, my son. Your grandfather was one of the last great Lakota warriors. The days of our glory have passed. The white man has driven us from our lands, and he has destroyed the mighty herds of buffalo, without which we cannot live."

He closed his eyes briefly for a moment before continuing: "The Wasichus say we must become farmers, like them. That we must slash the bosom of our Mother Earth with plows, and cut her living hair with scythes. That we—who used to ride the plains, free as eagles, following the buffalo—must now labor and sweat from the rising of the sun to its setting, to bring forth the white man's food."

He said that to me, son and grandson of great chiefs, who would be put in a pine box and buried deep in the white man's earth.

4

Jenny Muldoon

I was a nervous wreck at breakfast the first day of school, worrying that my new school would be like all the old ones: a bunch of kids who knew each other, with me on the outside, looking in.

"I'm sure you'll make friends, Jenny," Paul said, looking worried. He seemed to be taking his new job as father very seriously.

"Remember, Jenny," Mom said, "to *have* friends, you have to *be* a friend."

"Oh, yuck. Give me a break, Mom," I said, sticking my

tongue out and pretending to gag. "You say that every time I go off to a new school."

"Well . . . you'll be the prettiest girl in the class, anyway," Paul said in a voice that was a little too hearty and reassuring. "You look like a million dollars in that outfit."

It was nice of him to try to cheer me up, so I said, "Thanks, Paul. You might be a little prejudiced, but thanks anyway."

Actually, I'd wanted to wear jeans to school, so I wouldn't look like I was trying too hard, but Mom made me wear a skirt. It was navy and white, and I wore a red, square-necked T-shirt with it. I looked good, but would I fit in with the others?

No. Naturally not. The other girls wore—guess what?—jeans and tank tops. The sleeveless tops showed off their great tans. I felt pale and overdressed beside them.

The school building was long, wooden, and painted white, just like our quarters. And it had that same old-fashioned railed veranda on both levels. A bronze plaque over the main door said the bottom floor had once been the kitchen and dining facilities for the Indian school. The second floor, it said, had been offices and faculty supply rooms.

But now it was the Ulysses S. Grant Elementary School. Hip, hip, hooray. All the grades, kindergarten through eighth, were in the same building. There was no separate middle school or junior high on the post. The high school kids, Paul said, were bused to the nearest county high school.

I'd always gone to big schools before, where you didn't know all the kids in your grade because the classes were divided. This time my grade—eighth—was so small that we all fit into one classroom. No lockers. No having to change rooms for different classes. Just rows of desks and a big, dusty cloakroom with hooks and shelves. I felt like Laura Ingalls Wilder in *Little House on the Prairie.*

Our teacher, Ms. Cavell, was young and eager. This was her first year of teaching, she told us—as if we couldn't guess. She was small and slender and looked more like a high school girl than a teacher. She had dark hair and warm, brown eyes.

Root beer eyes, I thought. *Ms. Cavell has eyes like Dad's.*

Funny, but that was all I could remember about Dad now—those brown eyes looking out at me from behind his mask of wrapped gauze. Mom and I both had blue eyes, and Paul's were gray. I was glad Ms. Cavell had nice brown eyes so I wouldn't forget Dad.

I'd taken a seat in the back of the classroom, and I looked around to see what sort of kids I'd be with for the next nine months.

When Paul told Mom and me about his orders to Fort Sayers he'd said, "We'll be there for a long time. This is supposed to be a three-year—maybe even a four-year—tour of duty."

That was what he called it. A "tour of duty." I'd have to get used to army lingo now that I was officially an army brat.

"I think you're going to like it, Jenny," he'd added. "I understand there are lots of things on post for kids your age to do."

"Like what?" I asked suspiciously.

"Oh, things like tennis, softball, soccer . . ."

His voice trailed away when he saw the expression on my face. "Did I say something wrong?" he asked.

I shrugged. "I hate to tell you this, Paul," I said, " but I'm not much of a jockette. I don't like games where you're supposed to fight to the death over a stupid ball. I always wind up getting hurt."

I took a deep breath and hurried on. If we three were supposed to live together happily ever after, he'd better learn the worst about me right away. "I'm not even an outdoors person. Actually, I'm not much fun at all. I'm very dull, and I'm sort of a social misfit, and—"

"Misfit!" Mom echoed. "Really, Jenny, don't you think you're being—"

Paul said, "I don't think you're dull, Jenny. And I don't think you're a misfit."

I made a face.

"No," he said, shaking his head. "What I *do* think is that you're a sensitive, thoughtful girl who's smarter than most kids her age. But I've noticed that you worry too much. About everything. And that's got to stop, because now you have me to do the worrying for this family."

Family. For some crazy reason, I suddenly felt like crying.

Mom was looking at him in a goopy, adoring way.

"Will you remember that, Jenny?" he asked quietly.

"Yes, sir," I said, blinking back tears, hoping he hadn't seen them. "If you say so . . . Major Dad." Then I tossed him a smarty-pants salute and left the room before things between him and Mom started to get sickening.

I could see the backs of heads from where I sat in the classroom. I always sat in the back so I could watch the other kids without them watching me.

I counted the heads: twenty-two. Just the right-sized

class, not too big, not too small. Looking around, I wondered about cliques. There were always cliques in every grade, and I never fit into any of them.

The other kids looked like what you might expect in an eighth-grade classroom. Some of the girls were sitting in the front row, talking and giggling. They must have known each other from before.

I took a good look at the other girls, the nongigglers. A couple of them seemed nervous and uneasy, like they were new, too. Maybe I'd hit it lucky this time and find a kindred spirit. It was bound to happen someday. Maybe.

One or two of the boys had crazy-looking hair and big, baggy pants, but the rest wore ordinary haircuts and blue jeans. There wasn't a tattoo or nose ring in sight. That figured. This was a military post, and the fathers around here probably weren't big on personal fashion statements.

Ms. Cavell started talking right off about how great it was to see us, and how we were going to have this incredible year together, doing things and learning things. No wonder she was so skinny! With all that energy and enthusiasm, she was probably burning off a million calories a minute.

"Many of you have lived all over the world, as well as throughout the United States," she said. "The life of a military child is a richly textured one. I'm hoping this year that we will have the opportunity of sharing our experiences with each other."

She'd decorated the room with travel posters from foreign countries, and now she indicated them with a magnificent sweep of her arm. "Perhaps some of you have been to the places shown on these posters."

One of the gigglers raised her hand and pointed to the

picture of what looked like a fairy-tale castle on a mountain top.

"I've seen that one. In real life, I mean. It's Neuschwanstein Castle, and it's in Bavaria, and it was built by this king they called Mad Ludwig. He was supposed to be totally crazy or something."

"That's correct!" cried Ms. Cavell. "The king was Ludwig the Second, and he was eventually deposed for insanity. But he was a patron of the arts and was responsible for some beautiful pieces of architecture."

"We were stationed in Germany and traveled a lot on the weekends," the giggler added, blushing. "We saw all sorts of stuff over there." She blushed again and looked down and wiggled around a little in her chair.

"This is exactly the sort of cultural participation I'd hoped for," Ms. Cavell said, looking ecstatic. "Thank you . . . uh . . . now let me see, you are . . . what is your name?"

"Natalie," said the giggler. "Natalie Berenson."

Ms. Cavell glanced down quickly at a paper on her desk. "Since I'm new here and haven't yet connected names to faces, I've drawn up a seating chart to help me. If you will all please stand, I'll give you your new seating assignments."

School lasted only a couple of hours that first day. After we got our new seats and books and had our "Getting to Know You" time, when each of us had to stand up and tell something about ourselves, Ms. Cavell let us go home.

There were more new kids in my class than I'd realized. The gigglers had been stationed together before, so they knew each other but weren't exactly a clique, and they seemed okay when they got up and talked about themselves. I mean, they didn't act stuck-up or nasty or anything.

I was right about the girls I'd thought were new to the school. They were. One of them—Mary Helen Ramos—told the class that her mother wrote children's picture books. Ms. Cavell started to get excited about that, but she calmed down somewhat when Mary Helen told her that Mrs. Ramos hadn't actually *sold* one yet.

As for the guys—well, it was too soon to make up my mind about them. I'd been assigned a desk in the third row, right in front of this big redheaded boy named Arnold who kept kicking my chair. At first, I wondered if he was deliberately trying to annoy me, or if maybe he had an unfortunate nervous tic.

When it was Arnold's turn, he sauntered to the front of the room, turned around slowly, and said, "I'm Arnold Spitzer. Everybody knows that name. My father's the commanding general of Fort Sayers."

"Yes, Arnold," Ms. Cavell said with a tight smile. "Most of us know who the commanding general of Fort Sayers is, but right now we'd like to learn a little something about *you.*"

Arnold struck a weightlifter pose and flexed his muscles. "What can I say, Ms. Cavell? It's hard to be humble when you're perfect in every way."

"What a creep!" somebody muttered. It sounded like Natalie.

Ms. Cavell sighed. "All right, Arnold, you may return to your seat. I believe it's Jenny's turn next."

Arnold gave Natalie a dirty look as he passed her desk, but Ms. Cavell wasn't watching. At least, she pretended she wasn't.

I wasn't sure what to say about myself, so I tried to make it short and simple: I told them I was from California, that my father was dead, that my mother had remarried, and that this was my first time ever on an army post.

I was nervous, and when I get nervous I act real uptight and cold. I wondered what the others thought of me.

"Well, then," said Ms. Cavell when I returned to my seat. "We'll all have to do our best to see that Jenny feels welcome here, won't we, class?"

At that, Arnold kicked my chair. Hard.

I took the long way home. I wanted to see some of the post.

Paul had given me a small pamphlet about Fort Sayers that morning. It had a map of the post on the front page, so I knew I couldn't get lost.

The first building I came to looked like a small jail. It was low and windowless, and its walls were made of thick gray stone. The plaque out front said it was a GUARDHOUSE and that it had been built by English prisoners during the Revolutionary War.

I stepped inside and looked around. Nobody was there, and it was dark and spooky, lit only by a dim overhead bulb. The center area had been turned into a small museum with a few locked glass cases holding old uniforms and swords.

To the left and right of the museum were short, narrow halls, unevenly paved with the same stones that had been used for the walls. Each had one cell on either side. The guardhouse had four cells, then—four damp, windowless cubicles behind low wooden doors.

The place smelled of mildew . . . and something else. What? Misery, unhappiness, maybe . . . if things like that have a scent. I felt my arms break out in goosebumps, the way they do when I watch a creepy movie, and I got out of there as fast as I could.

I was ashamed of myself once I was standing in the sunshine again. What a scaredy cat! What crazy ideas! But it *had* been dark in there and I *was* alone. And those gloomy, moldy cells . . . I mean, that place would have spooked anybody.

A gravel pathway led past the guardhouse and beyond, to a row of tall pines. I decided to follow the path through the pines to see where it went. I wasn't ready to go home and face Mom yet. She'd be all over me with questions.

The grass on either side of the path was as neat and closely trimmed as a golf green. The bushes were pruned and mulched. Arnold's father must run a pretty classy post, I figured. Too bad he had such a nerdy son.

I went through the opening in the pines. The pathway ended at the gate to a small cemetery, surrounded by a rather ugly chain-link fence.

The gate squeaked as I pushed it open. Stepping inside, I found myself among row upon row of flat, white headstones. I'd seen pictures of Arlington National Cemetery, and these looked just like the military headstones on the graves there—straight, uniform, and impersonal.

But the names on those headstones! Mary Pretty Feather, Iroquois. James White Horse, Sioux. Amos Young Wolf, Navajo. Indian names, all of them, with dates of birth and death that showed them to be children, most of them not yet in their teens. So many of them! And they'd all died in the late 1800s. Surely there were too many graves for such a short time. I mean, schoolkids just didn't die like that, even in those days, did they?

What could have happened to them?

Let's see . . . the late 1800s. The Civil War had recently ended, and settlers were moving westward in covered wagons, fighting the Indians. I remembered all the western movies I'd seen, with the wagons drawn up in a circle and the Indians riding around and around them, whooping and hollering and shooting flaming arrows.

I thought about the children, resting so quietly here beneath the white stones. Those whooping, hollering Indians had been their fathers or grandfathers. And then these kids had been sent here to be students at the Indian school.

James White Horse, Sioux. The Sioux were up in the Dakotas. That much I knew.

Amos Young Wolf, Navajo. The Navajos were in Arizona and New Mexico.

They were all a long way from home.

How'd they get here? By train? Yes, they had trains in those days. They would have been taken from their families and tipis and villages and put on a train—that must have scared the liver out of them—and then sent halfway across the United States to what surely must have seemed like an alien planet.

How lonely and frightened they must have been, cut off from everything they'd ever known. And what did they die of? I'd read somewhere that the Indians had no resistance to measles and chicken pox and things like that when they first came in contact with the white man. Was that what caused all those small graves with the silent tombstones? Or was it homesickness? Did they just pine away?

I knew all about homesickness. Mom had sent me to summer camp one year. I'd cried myself to sleep every night—and that camp was only thirty miles from home.

In one corner of the cemetery, the long branch of a pine tree trailed over the fence and rested on one of the tombstones. It bothered me to see it like that. It was like a heavy arm pressing down on the tomb.

I moved toward it, careful to step between the graves, not on them. The headstone on the grave in the corner read:

JONAH FLYING CLOUD
SIOUX
BORN 1867
DIED 1880

I hated to do it, but I had to step on the gently mounded grave to remove the branch that lay across the headstone. As I threw the branch back over the fence, I suddenly felt so wobbly that I had to cling to the headstone for a couple of seconds until I was strong enough to stagger away and sink down on the grass beside the grave.

I put my hand on my forehead, wondering if I was coming down with something. A virus, maybe.

The sun was hot on my back, warming me. It felt good. A cricket chirped beside the fence. The weak feeling passed, and soon I was fine again.

I stood up and brushed the grass off my skirt, thinking: *It's lunchtime. I'm starving-to-death hungry. That's why I felt so woozy just now. And that creepy guardhouse—and these sad little graves. Starting a new school's bad enough without all that.*

Yes, that was probably it. The first day at a new school was always hard, and I'd been too nervous to sleep much last night. I was tired. I was hungry. And then all this death and dying stuff . . .

I went home by the road that made a big circle around

the parade ground. According to my map, it passed Quarters One, the home of the commanding general. Oh, yuck. Arnold's house.

Quarters One looked like a scaled-down version of something out of *Gone with the Wind,* with four tall columns and a wide veranda. Very impressive. No wonder Arnold was so hung up on himself.

The front door was open, and, as I passed, a sort of whooping, sobbing sound came from inside. It was either a sob or a scream. And then I heard a shrill voice yelling, "Arnold! Arnold!"

The door was immediately slammed shut. It had one of those big oval glass windows in it, and, as it closed, I saw a flash of red hair. Arnold! He peered out at me through the glass and made a terrible face, his mouth moving. I think he was swearing at me.

Who'd made that whooping noise? And then why did Arnold act like he was mad at *me?*

What a dork!

For some reason, I felt better now about attending the Ulysses S. Grant Elementary School. For once, at least, *I* wouldn't be the weirdest kid in my class.

5

Jonah Flying Cloud

The Lakota word for "children" is *wakanyeja,* which means "the sacred ones." We were cherished and loved.

Our elders treated us with respect. We were never slapped or scolded. If an adult of our tribe had ever struck a child, it would have been considered an act of unspeakable brutality.

The Wasichus believed differently. "To spare the rod is to spoil the child," Mr. Samuel said, "especially with Indian children, who are savage, uncivilized, and in need of correction."

He spoke those words when we were all still new at the school and did not yet understand the white man's language. When the interpreter told us what Mr. Samuel had said, we looked at each other in puzzlement. It was civilized to beat children? What kind of people were these white men?

"That must be why the Wasichus tell so many lies, then," Swift Running River said. "The truth is beaten out of them when they are young."

The interpreter put his finger to his lips in warning. "Take care, Swift Running River. That kind of talk could get you into big trouble."

Swift Running River only laughed. "My father, who died fighting Custer Long Hair, always told me: 'Meet your death on the battlefield, my son. That is the way of the true Lakota.' "

"This isn't a battlefield, Swift Running River," the interpreter said sternly. "It's a school. You are here to learn the white man's ways, not to fight him."

"You are wrong," said Swift Running River. "They will try to kill us in this place. You will see. And I will fight bravely—and to the death—when they do."

The same interpreter, Mr. Baker, who'd learned our language through the Indian agency, was with us when we got our Wasichu names. These were taken from their Good Book. I did not like my name, Jonah, because it was the name of a man who had been swallowed by a big fish. I begged them to change it, but the teacher said it was a good name, and so I let them call me Jonah.

It was different with Swift Running River.

The teacher made quick, flowing marks on the writing board with her chalk. "This is your new name, your Good Book name," she told Swift Running River through the interpreter. "Your name is now Job. Your last name will be your father's name, Many Horses—"

"Job?" interrupted Swift Running River, narrowing his eyes suspiciously. "I do not like the short sound of that. It sounds like the barking of a sick dog. What does it mean? Who was this man, Job? What did he do that his name is written in the Wasichu Good Book?"

The teacher replied and Mr. Baker quickly translated: "Job was a man of great virtue who was smitten with terrible sores and boils and pustules all over his body from his scalp to his feet. And then he—"

"Sores and boils?" shouted Swift Running River. His face was as dark as a thunder cloud. "Sores and boils? You are giving me the name of a man who bears upon his body the marks of shame? The marks that indicate I have violated the untouchable?"

The teacher, an older lady with a face like a rabbit, was dumbstruck at Swift Running River's shouting. She stood as if frozen before her writing board, still holding her Good Book. Her pale eyes were circles of fear as Swift Running River began to pace up and down before her, shaking his fist.

She uttered a little cry, like the bleating of a calf buffalo, and looked to Mr. Baker for help. Mr. Baker looked to me.

"What does he mean?" Mr. Baker asked me, almost in a whisper.

"Do you know nothing, white man?" roared Swift Running River before I could reply. "Have your people no purity? No shame?"

"I . . . I do not understand," said Mr. Baker.

I tried to explain. "When a young maiden of our tribe has her first flowing . . . that which makes her a woman and able to bear children . . . the products of it are wrapped in a bundle and hidden, so that no evil spirit—*tonwan*—can find it and make mischief with it."

I paused, so that I could choose my words carefully. "But if any man should . . . meddle . . . with such a bundle, he would be plagued with boils and sores. Our people would shun him. He would be thought lower than a coyote."

The interpreter translated hurriedly, his eyes flicking back and forth between Swift Running River, me, and the teacher.

Swift Running River stopped pacing and glared at the teacher, drawing his lips back from his teeth like a snarling wolf. "You have defiled me. You have dishonored me with that name!"

The anger in his voice frightened even me. When Mr. Baker explained Swift Running River's last words, the teacher spun around and used her sleeve to erase the marks on the board. "Wait, wait! The matter is quickly remedied. I'll give you another name! A better one! Let's see . . ."

She ruffled through the pages of the Good Book. Her hands trembled as she wrote the new name on the board. "There!" she cried. "I'm sure you will approve of this one."

"What does she write?" Swift Running River demanded.

"She writes the name Elijah," said Mr. Baker.

"What does the Good Book say about this man Elijah? Is it a good name?"

"Yes, it's a very good name. Elijah was a great and powerful prophet, a wise man."

"How did he die?"

Mr. Baker said, "He was carried up to the heavens in a flaming chariot. A chariot is a war wagon, very fast, with only two wheels."

Swift Running River nodded thoughtfully. "To be taken up to Wanagi Yata in a flaming war wagon is a good thing. *Hau.* Yes. I will let you call me by his name. Elijah is a good luck name."

Swift Running River's victory in the matter of the naming made him more boastful than ever. The older boys now would have nothing to do with him. They could not bear his strutting and bragging.

As a result, Swift Running River—now known to the Wasichus as Elijah Many Horses—stayed around me all the time. There was no ridding myself of him. I asked myself what my father would do, and my answer was that my father would assume responsibility for Swift Running River, unpleasant though he was, because he was a member of our band. As the son of the chief, my duty was clear. I must look out for Swift Running River.

Two mornings after the naming, word was passed that a group of Wasichu men, carrying sharp cutting tools and razors, had come inside the school grounds. They had come to cut off our hair, it was said, our long hair, the symbol of health, virtue, pride, tradition—everything that mattered to our people.

"*Pahin Kaksa! Pahin Kaksa!* They are cutting the hair!"

The cry rang out down the halls and across the parade

field. The children ran in all directions, pursued by their teachers.

I rushed for the safety of my dormitory room. Behind me as I ran I could hear Swift Running River shouting, "They are going to kill us! Stand fast and resist them!"

I should have stayed and told him they wanted his hair, not his life, but I was intent on escape. Reaching my dormitory, I crawled under my bed to hide. The Wasichus could not have my hair. Cutting it would bring disgrace to me and my ancestors. Cutting the hair was only allowed when mourning the death of a loved one.

I know of what happened next only through the tellings of others.

The children were rounded up and herded into the dining hall, where the men with the cutting tools and razors awaited.

Swift Running River, who had been borne along with the crowd, now leapt up on one of the tables where we took our meals. We had not yet been given our white man's clothing, so Swift Running River still wore his Lakota leggings and shirt.

Whipping a knife from his waistband, he held it aloft and shouted: "We will all soon be dead. They plan to kill us!"

The younger children started to cry when he said that, but Swift Running River held up his hand for silence. "They will not take my hair," he cried. "They wish to scalp us and steal our spirits. I will not let them do this thing. I, myself, will cut it as a sign of mourning!"

Before anyone could stop him, he had sliced through his long braids, all the time singing, "*Hoka hey! Hoka hey!* It is a good day to die!"

This is what Lakota warriors sing when they go off to battle. That was what Swift Running River's father had sung when he rode away to fight Custer Long Hair.

"Stop that, you fool!" shouted Mr. Samuel, who was with the hair-cutting men. "Get down from there! Nobody's going to die. We're only going to cut your hair and treat you for head lice."

Still singing, Swift Running River slashed his arms with his knife, another sign of mourning. Then he gashed his face. "*Hoka hey! Hoka hey!*" The blood ran down his face onto his shirt. It dripped off his arms and made puddles on the table. Those watching told me later that even the hair-cutting Wasichus backed away in alarm.

Mr. Samuel hopped upon a chair and then onto the table where Swift Running River stood. He held a leather strap in his hand. Everyone knew what that was. It was what the white men used to punish their children. They beat them with things like that. None of us had yet been beaten with it, but the very sight of it made us fearful.

Swift Running River stopped singing and watched through narrowed eyes as Mr. Samuel slowly approached him down the length of the table.

"Put that knife down, son, and take your punishment like a man," Mr. Samuel said, raising the strap. "It will be easier on you if you do as I say."

Swift Running River did not understand the words, but the gesture clearly showed what Mr. Samuel planned to do to him.

Dropping into a half crouch, Swift Running River waited, his knife at the ready. He held his braids in his other hand, and swung them back and forth, teasing Mr. Samuel.

Then he laughed and threw down his knife, flinging his

braids after it. In one bound, he closed with Mr. Samuel, grabbed him by the shirt, and pushed him backward off the table.

Mr. Samuel twisted as he fell in an effort to save himself, and landed on his face. His nose was bleeding when he rose, but that did not stop him. Reaching up, he seized Swift Running River by the legs and dragged him to the ground.

Signaling for the hair-cutting men to hold the boy down, he ripped off Swift Running River's shirt and began to beat him with the leather strap. Swift Running River was large for his age and strong, and it took four Wasichus to keep him from fighting back.

When he was finished, Mr. Samuel said, "Take him to the guardhouse. A couple of days on bread and water ought to cool him down."

They told me afterward that Swift Running River had not flinched or shed a tear throughout the beating. And that, as he was taken off to the guardhouse, his head was high and he was chanting a Lakota song of victory.

They found me under my bed and dragged me out and cut my hair, along with everyone else's. They put purple medicine on our heads after the hair-cutting. They said it was to kill the bugs that lived on our heads, but that was not true. We had no bugs on our heads. The Wasichus only did it to show us that we were dirty savages who needed civilizing.

After supper, I slipped out of the dormitory and made my way in the darkness to the guardhouse. I moved with great stealth. If I were caught, Mr. Samuel would beat me, just as he had beaten Swift Running River.

There were no windows on the outside of the guardhouse,

so I could not call in to Swift Running River. I waited and watched from behind a tree until I was sure there were no guards about. Then I slipped through the door.

A candle burned on the table in the center room. On either side of the room was a short hall. I picked up the candle and stepped into the one on the right.

There was a cell on each side of the hall. The doors on both of them were ajar, so I knew Swift Running River was not being kept in either one.

He was in the other side. I found his cell. There was a little barred window in the door, and I held up the candle and looked in at him.

He was huddled in a corner. I called to him.

"Go away," he said.

"Are you all right, Swift Running River?"

"Yes. Go away."

"What you did was a brave thing," I told him.

"I should have killed him when I had the chance," said Swift Running River.

"You did the right thing," I said. "It would have been wrong to kill Mr. Samuel."

"No. I should have killed him instead of letting him beat me. No Wasichu will ever beat me again. I am a Lakota. My father was a brave warrior. I am not a dog to be kicked and beaten."

"Here," I said. "I brought you something to eat." I pushed the piece of bread and meat I'd saved from my supper through the opening in the bars.

"I'm not hungry," he said.

"Eat, Swift Running River. You will need your strength. You held your head high when you went into this cell. You must also hold it high when you come out."

That was the first time I saw the spirit-ghost of the white girl. As I turned to leave the guardhouse, I saw her standing in the center room, looking toward me.

She was like a wisp of smoke, and she wavered and shimmered in the candlelight. She had long pale hair, and her clothing was strange, even for a Wasichu.

I had never seen a spirit-ghost before, although my grandmother had told me about them many times. She said that no harm comes of seeing a ghost, unless it is singing a death song.

This one did not sing, but she looked afraid. I could sense her fear. And although she was looking straight at me, I could tell she did not see me. That made me feel brave and bold.

What was she afraid of? Did she know somehow that I was there, watching her? Or was she able to see Swift Running River sitting alone and in despair in his dark cell?

As I watched, she faded into nothingness, the way a wisp of smoke vanishes when the wind blows.

I was to see the girl spirit-ghost several times before I died.

I wondered who she was and from what faraway place she had come. And why she had been sent to haunt me.

6

Jenny Muldoon

Mom and Paul peppered me with questions at supper. Did I like school? Did I make any friends? What was my teacher like?

Two pairs of anxious eyes, peering at me across the table.

I did my best to act cheerful and normal. Acting normal is always hard for me.

"The commanding general's son is in my class," I said, trying to make conversation. "His name is Arnold."

"Really?" Mom said, perking right up. "I saw his mother when I was shopping in the post exchange this morning. I heard someone call her by name. She's a beautiful woman—tall and slim with masses of gorgeous red hair."

"Oh, so that's where Arnold gets it. His red hair, I mean," I said. "But on him it's not gorgeous. It makes him look like a great big carrot. Arnold Spitzer is a total, absolute creep."

"I do hope you're not going to be supercritical of your classmates again this time, Jenny." Mom gave me one of her stern parental stares. "It wouldn't hurt, you know, to start off on the right foot for a change. Be friendly. Keep an open mind."

"What do you mean?" I demanded. "I can't help it if the other kids don't like me!"

Mom sighed and shook her head. "Maybe you can. You know, Jenny, you've got a real attitude. That chip you carry on your shoulder is as big as the Rock of Gibraltar. Sometimes you scare even me, and I'm your mother, God help me."

I shrugged and rolled my eyes. Mom hates it like crazy when I roll my eyes, so I did it again, just in case she missed it the first time.

"Jenny . . ." she said in a warning voice.

"Maureen, darling," Paul said hastily before Mom could launch into one of her lectures. "These scalloped potatoes are the greatest! May I please have another helping?"

Even though I was dead tired, I had trouble getting to sleep that night. I kept thinking about that sad little graveyard, and all the tombstones with the names of Indian children on them.

My room was upstairs, and at the end of the hall. The windows went from floor to ceiling and opened out onto the upper veranda. The ceilings were high on this floor. Well, no wonder. The children had needed plenty of fresh air. After all, hadn't this once been the school infirmary?

Infirmary, as in hospital.

And people die in hospitals!

I sat bolt upright in bed and snapped on the light. Those kids—those dead little Indian kids—some of them, no *all* of them, must have died here, in this very room!

I looked around, trying to visualize it as it must have been in those days. There was a small study between my room and Mom and Paul's. At one time, the three rooms probably had been one big hospital ward.

No, wait a minute. What was I thinking? They wouldn't have put boys and girls together in one room. The study must have been the nurse's station, and it probably had doors—now walled over—that opened into both rooms, with the boys on one side and the girls on the other.

Little white metal beds, all in a row. I could almost see them lined up along that wall over there, facing the windows. Little metal tables beside them. Holding what? What kind of medicine did they have back then? None of the modern miracle drugs, that's for sure, judging by all those tombstones out there.

I pulled the sheet up under my chin. It was eerie knowing that I was sleeping in the same room where somebody had . . . A sudden gust of wind rattled my window, and my heart nearly stopped. If any place in the world deserved to be haunted, it was here—right *here*—where all those kids had died.

I finally worked up the nerve to turn off my bedside light, but not before I'd piled up my pillows so that I would be sleeping practically upright, ready to jump up and run.

All through that long night, I kept waking up, expecting to see at my bedside the pale, sad face of a little Indian ghost. Hands outstretched. Hollow cheeks. Big dark eyes.

No ghost appeared, but in the morning I was the one with big dark eyes. I had such black circles under my eyes that I looked like a raccoon.

Great. Some impression I'd make on the kids in my class. Well, maybe they'd think I was an endangered species and feel sorry for me.

Yeah. Sure.

I was late for school that morning because I spent a lot of time trying to do something about those dark circles. I tried putting ice-cube compresses on them, but that only turned my skin red and white in a splotchy, polka-dot effect. I yelled for Mom, and she had me lie down with a warm washcloth over my eyes to get rid of the freaky splotching.

Anyway, what with one thing and the other—my hysterics and Mom trying to shut me up and make me look human again—Ms. Cavell was already at her desk and everybody was quieting down when I bolted through the door, five minutes late and panting like a runaway horse.

Arnold Spitzer was sitting up ramrod straight at his desk,

feet where they belonged, his red hair wet and slicked back. I should have known he was up to something rotten when he greeted me with a big, smarmy smile.

"Jenny, Jenny, bright as a penny," he said, waggling his head at me like the fool that he was.

I dropped into my seat and squirmed around, removing my backpack.

Our desks were dark and old-fashioned looking. The top lifted up to reveal a good-sized storage area for books and papers. There was also extra room for books and other stuff beneath the seat in a sort of metal bin thing that opened on the left. You had to hang sideways out of your seat to get at it.

I finally got my backpack off and leaned over to put it under my seat.

And then I saw . . . it.

A gray mouse, limp and dead, lying under my desk.

I hung there—half out of my seat, half in, paralyzed with fear and loathing.

I hate mice. A lot of people are scared of snakes and spiders, but with me it's mice. Especially dead ones. I was too grossed out to scream.

So there I hung, staring at that thing, while behind me Arnold snorted and laughed. He'd done it, the creep. He'd put that dead mouse under my desk.

I might have stayed horizontal forever, long hair sweeping the floor, eyes bulging with horror at that dead mouse, if Mary Helen Ramos hadn't looked over—she was directly across the aisle from me—and let out a shriek that split the air like a clap of thunder.

"Mouse! Mouse!" she yelled, pointing.

That did it. There was screaming of a sort that had not been heard since the sinking of the *Titanic*.

Obviously, this situation had never been covered in any of Ms. Cavell's teaching manuals, but she handled it like a pro. After she got the girls to sit back down and stop screaming, she appealed to the boys. "Could one of you please get rid of that mouse for me?"

Ms. Cavell had no trouble finding somebody to do the job. A couple of them practically fought over who'd get the honor of dragging the mouse from under my desk by the tail and dumping it into the plastic bag that Ms. Cavell, head averted, held out at arm's length.

The job fell to Dwayne Larson. You'd think he'd just been named Man of the Year. He made a real production of it, too, like somebody in one of those PBS animal habitat specials.

Afterward, Ms. Cavell acted like she thought the mouse had crawled under my desk and died from natural causes. But I knew better. I knew it was horrible old Arnold Spitzer who'd found it and put it there.

First chance I got, I turned around in my seat and gave him a hateful look. "I know what you did, Arnold, and I'm going to get you for that."

Arnold opened his eyes wide and tried to look innocent. "Me? What have I done?"

"You know perfectly well, sicko! You put that mouse under my desk, didn't you?"

He only laughed.

"Mess with me, Arnold," I warned from between clenched teeth, "and I will destroy you."

That made him laugh even harder.

Later that morning, Ms. Cavell announced she was giving us a long-term history assignment: a research paper on a historical person, place, or event of our own choosing.

"You may team up with someone for the research, if you like," she said, "but you must both put in an equal effort."

Ms. Cavell gave us overnight to choose our subjects, but some of us knew right away what we wanted to write about. She went around the classroom and noted our choices in a little black notebook.

When she got to me, I said, "I'd like to find out more about the Fort Sayers Indian School. I was out walking around yesterday and I found the cemetery. There are a lot of kids my—our—age buried there and, well, I'd like to do my research paper on the school and what it must have been like for them."

"Wonderful!" said Ms. Cavell, scribbling away in her notebook. "The post library ought to be a good source of information about the Indian school. I'll be looking forward to reading your paper, Jenny."

Behind me, Arnold bounced around noisily in his seat and called out, "Me, too, me, too, Ms. Cavell. That's what I want to write about!"

"But I don't want to do it with Arnold," I said desperately. "I want to do it by myself."

Ms. Cavell chewed on the end of her pen. "Ah . . . is there any special reason you want this project rather than another one, Arnold?"

"Sure there is," Arnold replied. "My father's the commanding general of Fort Sayers. I ought to know everything I can about it, don't you think?"

"Well, Jenny, Arnold does have a point there," said Ms. Cavell. "And perhaps Arnold's father could help you get access to some additional information about the subject."

"That's right," said Arnold. "My old man's in charge of everything and everybody around here."

"That isn't exactly how I meant it, Arnold," said Ms. Cavell, looking distressed, "but he—your father—would undoubtedly be of great help to you and your project. And our entire class could learn a great deal about the base and its history from your research."

For a minute I considered changing my subject. Anything would be better than working with Arnold. And then I thought—*No, he's not going to make me quit. This is my project. I thought of it first. I'll make him work so hard he'll be sorry he joined up with me.*

So when Ms. Cavell asked me, "Is it all right with you, then, Jenny, if Arnold shares your project?" I was able to answer—although sullenly—"Yes, Ms. Cavell. I guess so. As long as he does his fair share."

After school I caught up with Arnold on the lawn. Grabbing his arm, I swung him around to face me and demanded, "Now what are you trying to pull, Spitzer? What's this partner stuff? You know I hate your guts."

"Boy, you sure do look like an old witch when you're mad, Muldoon," he replied.

"Why do you want to join up with me on this assignment?" I demanded. "How come I get stuck with you?"

"Relax," he said. "Nothing personal intended. It's just that I figured it's a good excuse to find out more about the murder."

"Murder? What are you talking about?"

"Aha!" Arnold said with a smirk. "See? I already know more about this project than you do."

"Are you flat-out crazy or what?"

"There was a murder here, years ago, when this was an Indian school," he said. "One of the Indian students killed somebody. I'd like to find out more about it."

"Murder?" I echoed. "There was a murder here at the Indian school?"

"Yeah," he said. "And this project gives us the chance to snoop."

He looked me up and down like he was checking me out and was not thrilled with what he saw. "You know, you're definitely not my type, Muldoon. You're one of those snooty ice maidens who think they're better than everybody else. I knew that the minute I laid eyes on you. But you're smart. The two of us, working together, could do a good job on this project. Okay?"

Snooty ice maiden? Me? I tried to think of a really sharp, cutting comeback to that one, but couldn't. Not on such short notice, anyway.

"Okay?" he repeated.

"Okay," I said, giving him a dirty look. "But remember this, Arnold. You do your fair share on this project or you're out."

Arnold held out his hands and pretended they were shaking. "Oooh, you scare me. I promise I'll be good—cross my heart and hope to die, stick a poker in my eye."

"Don't give me any violent ideas," I said, turning on my heel and leaving him standing there looking dumb with his hands still stuck out.

Well, at least I'd had the last word, even if it was only to a creep like Arnold "It's Hard to be Humble When You're Perfect in Every Way" Spitzer.

7

Jonah Flying Cloud

We were always hungry at school.

We ate three small meals a day, with nothing allowed in between. The hands on the faces of the school clocks had to be in a certain position, and bells had to ring, before we were marched silently and in straight lines, like Wasichu soldiers, into the dining room. Then, at another bell, we sat down on hard chairs at a long table. We were required to eat in a special manner using knives and forks. It took us a long time to learn to use the forks. We had never seen anything like them before. At home we dipped into our food with our fingers, but that was not the civilized way to eat, they told us.

At first, we did not like the white man's food, but hunger taught us to be grateful for what was put on our plates, even though it did not satisfy us or fill us up. We were not allowed to refill our plates, and most of us were still hungry when we left the table. Some nights we could not get to sleep, we were that hungry. It is hard to sleep when your stomach is empty.

We endured it as best we could, but then some of the older boys began stealing to keep from going hungry.

Swift Running River told me how it was done. "Behind the kitchen is a large vegetable garden with a wooden fence around it. When the workers have left the kitchen at night, the boys crawl over the fence and get into the garden."

"No one sees them do it?" I asked.

"No," he said, his lips a thin, bitter line. "They are good at it. Indians are supposed to be thieving savages, remember?"

Swift Running River told me the boys dug potatoes from the ground, sometimes turnips and carrots. "So far, the white man cook hasn't missed them. He is lazy and does a poor job of digging them up. Much of it would only rot in the ground, anyway, the way he works."

"But it is dangerous," I said, thinking of the leather strap. "They will be punished if Mr. Samuel catches them."

Swift Running River moved his shoulders, as if remembering the feel of the blows upon his back, and said nothing.

He had changed since his two days in the guardhouse. Gone were his boastful ways and arrogant swagger. There was something dark, dangerous, and brooding in his eyes now.

When I asked him why he did not try to run away since he hated the school so much, he replied, "I am brave, but I am no fool, son of Flying Cloud. We are many sleeps away from home. I have no horse. Nothing to trade or barter for food. I do not wish to become another white man's slave."

Swift Running River still used words like *sleeps* for "nights" and *moons* for "months," even though the rest of us were beginning to change over to the white man's names for them. It was his way of holding on to his Lakota heritage, I think.

"Also," he said, "I have seen how they treat runaways. They chain them like animals in those cells. I would die before I let anyone put chains on me."

He lowered his voice and looked around to make sure no

one was listening. "And there is something else, son of Flying Cloud. I am speaking of this only to you, and you must keep silent about it. I will never go back to one of those cells, because they are haunted. A spirit-ghost appeared to me when I was there."

He went on to tell me it had been a Wasichu ghost, a girl with long pale hair. "It was very strange," he said. "I could see her, but she could not see me."

I listened but said nothing. I do not know why I held my tongue. Perhaps it was because if I told him that I, too, had seen the ghost of the Wasichu girl, it might form a brother-bond between us, and I did not wish to become brothers with Swift Running River.

Swift Running River decided to steal potatoes because of Johnny Little Fox.

Johnny Little Fox was also of our band and our village. Like all the other students, he had been given a Good Book name to go with his Lakota name. His Good Book name was John, but the teachers called him Johnny. They said that Johnny was the shorter, more friendly way of saying his name. This puzzled us, since "Johnny" took longer to say than "John," and since when did the teachers wish to become our friends? But the ways of the Wasichus always puzzled us, so we did not question them about this.

Little Fox was nine years old, and small and thin for his age. Lately, though, he had started to shoot upward in height and was hungry all the time.

For some reason, Little Fox looked upon Swift Running River as a hero. Maybe it was because the older boy had acted like a Lakota warrior the day of the hair-cutting. Or maybe it was because Swift Running River was kind to him. The one thing the little ones missed most was the kindness and love they'd been given by their families and the members of their village. There was none of that here, only discipline and harshness and threats of punishment.

When I saw Swift Running River sneaking bits of his meals out of the dining hall and giving them to Little Fox, I was ashamed. I was already long-legged and well grown, bigger and stronger than others my age. Little Fox needed the extra pieces of bread and meat more than I did. I should have been aware of my responsibilities to him earlier, without having to look to Swift Running River for guidance.

At first it was painful to eat even less than before, but I reminded myself that when my voice changed, signaling manhood, by Lakota custom I would be of an age to fast and prepare myself for my Vision Quest—the time when I would go up on the mountain to pray and listen to the spirit voices and receive the vision that would govern my life.

I was a long way from my mountain, but I hoped my fasting and sacrifice now might make the holy spirits look upon me with favor and remember my good deeds when I returned home to my people.

Swift Running River said he would be the one to climb over the fence and gather the potatoes. Johnny Little Fox and I would stand guard and make a bird-whistle sound if someone approached.

We waited until everyone had settled down for the night. We put pillows under our blankets, to look like sleeping bodies, in case anyone checked our beds. Then we crept noiselessly from our dormitories, taking care not to awaken anyone. That part was exciting. I felt like a Lakota warrior, raiding an enemy camp.

Little Fox and I waited in the darkness while Swift Running River crawled over the fence and disappeared on the other side. We had decided not to take too many potatoes this first time, in case they might be missed. Swift Running River wore his school trousers with many pockets. He told us he would return when he had filled them. "That should give us enough for a feast," he said.

The second—and most important—part of the raid was cooking the potatoes. Eating them raw was hard on the stomach. I had talked to some of the older boys who had stolen from the garden before, and they told me how they cooked their potatoes.

"Beneath the school kitchen is a place called the 'boiler room,'" they said. "It is always unlocked because there is nothing in there but a great metal container, the 'boiler,' where water is heated by a coal furnace until it is as hot as the Wasichu Bad Place they tell us about in church. Then it travels through long pipes up to the kitchen, where it comes out in great streams to be used for the washing of the dishes."

I had never heard of such a thing as a boiler, so I listened attentively. "But what if someone—one of the Wasichus—comes in and finds us?" I asked. "Surely the boiler needs to be tended throughout the night."

"No, it doesn't," was the reply. "After supper, one of the workmen fills the furnace with coal and closes it tightly. "He doesn't return because the water in the boiler will stay hot until morning."

The oldest boy, Running Wolf, went on to explain that if

we laid the potatoes on the top of the boiler, they cooked through very quickly.

"We have also parched corn and cooked turnips that way," he said. "These Wasichu teachers would starve us to death if they could. They eat the best of everything and give us what is left over. I found a maggot in my oatmeal this morning, but I was hungry, so I fished it out and ate the oatmeal anyway."

The boiler was still red-hot when we crept in from the garden. I nearly burned my fingers laying the stolen potatoes in a row across its top—the hottest part—to cook.

The boiler made strange sounds, as if a devil was inside, trying to get out. But what did we know? None of us had ever seen a boiler before. We figured something had to strain mightily and noisily in order to heat the water and send it surging up through the pipes into the kitchen.

The potatoes began to cook very quickly, sending out wonderful scents. Johnny Little Fox stared at them, his mouth making water the way a starving dog's does when it sees meat.

I turned the potatoes, to keep them from burning. The boiler was so hot I had to stand back and reach my arms out at full length to do so. I hoped they would cook quickly, because Little Fox kept asking me, over and over again, when they would be done.

"They will be ready soon," I said. "Be patient, Little Fox. They are almost soft enough to eat."

The boiler was making louder noises now—shaking, shuddering noises—and growing hotter. The metal glowed red.

There was a sudden frightening hiss, and a thick white cloud of steam shot out from one of the pipes, where it was joined to another. If we had been standing in front it it, we would have been burned. We jumped back, away from the hissing pipe, and stared fearfully at each other.

The boiler rumbled and began to shake with a great violence.

Swift Running River was the first to move. "Run!" he shouted, seizing Little Fox's arm and dragging him toward the door. I followed close behind.

The doorway to the boiler room was low and narrow. We had to duck our heads to run out into the night. I was behind Little Fox. I pushed and shoved him, and stumbled through the doorway behind him, slamming the heavy wooden door shut behind me.

We were safe. The thick stone walls of the boiler room now separated us from the raging monster inside.

"My potato!" cried Little Fox. "My potato is in there!"

Before either Swift Running River or I could stop him, he ran back inside.

Another great rumble, another hissing of steam . . . and the sound of Little Fox screaming . . . screaming . . . and then his screams were drowned out by a mighty blast, louder than the strike of a thunderbolt, and of such power that the windows of the kitchen above us blew outward, showering Swift Running River and me with broken glass.

Then, at last, silence.

At first, I could not hear. I saw Swift Running River's lips moving, saying something, but it sounded like a low hum.

"Little Fox!" I cried, although I could barely hear my own voice. "Where is Little Fox?"

The door to the boiler room lay on the ground. Its hinges had been broken in the blast. Swift Running River entered first. I tried to follow him, but he stood in the doorway, unmoving. I looked past him into the room.

The boiler was no longer there. Overhead was a large hole, where the boiler had blown up through the ceiling and into the kitchen. Water was running from a broken pipe in the wall, flooding the floor.

The furnace door had been blown open. The burning coals lit up the room.

Little Fox lay in a small, bloody heap where he'd been thrown by the force of the blast. We did not have to go over to him to see that he was dead. His eyes were open, but they were staring and unseeing. His arms and legs were twisted and bent in the wrong directions. The smell of seared flesh was strong.

And in one hand, one broken, scalded hand, Johnny Little Fox still clutched his potato.

Swift Running River did not come to the burial. I do not know where he hid when we were all being lined up and marched to the little cemetery at the far side of the parade field.

Everyone had to attend, even those who did not know Johnny Little Fox. Mr. Samuel preached to us at great length about Little Fox's death being the will of the Wasichu god, but he preached even longer about the stealing of the potatoes.

"The wages of sin is death," he said, his eyes flashing.

Mr. Samuel always spoke for his god, as if the two of them ruled the world together. But surely the Wasichu god was more merciful than Mr. Samuel. Little Fox had been young and hungry. He'd given his life for a potato. No god, anywhere, would condemn a child for that.

So many children had died at the school that Mr. Samuel had set aside this piece of land for a burying ground. A low fence, painted white, surrounded it. Over each grave was a wooden cross to mark its place.

And yet as I watched, while Mr. Samuel's voice droned on and on, the burying ground wavered and changed before my eyes.

No longer was it surrounded by a wooden fence. It was now enclosed by one made of great links of a strange, pale metal. And there were so many graves! Rows and rows of them. Flat stone markers had replaced the wooden crosses.

In the corner of the cemetery, something moved: a wisp of mist that shimmered and twisted and then formed itself into a shape, a human shape—the shape of the pale-haired Wasichu girl I had seen in the guardhouse.

She seemed intent on lifting the trailing branch of a pine tree from one of the headstones.

It was too far away for me to see the name on the headstone, too far away to see the dates of the birth and death. And yet, somehow, I knew whose grave it was.

It was mine.

I was the one buried in the grave beneath the pine tree.

8

Jenny Muldoon

At first I thought I was imagining things.

I was up in my room, sitting at my desk, trying to figure

out how to start my history project, when it happened. Something dark moved—just the merest flicker of movement—in the far corner of the room. When I glanced over, nothing was there. I looked away, and it happened again. Nothing moved when I stared directly into the corner, but the moment I looked away, there it was again, that motion that I could see only out of the corner of my eye.

I rubbed my eyes with my knuckles. Was I going blind? Or crazy?

I got up and walked over to the corner. What was doing that moving? A hanging spiderweb, maybe, stirring in a draft?

No spiderwebs, but I felt a deep, penetrating cold, as if I were standing in front of an open refrigerator. But it was only here, in this one spot. When I stepped into the middle of the room again, the chilly feeling disappeared.

The incredible part is, I wasn't afraid. Not at all. Last night I'd nearly freaked out, thinking about the Indian students who'd died in this room. But tonight was different. Because those Indian kids were my project now, I was starting to feel like an investigative reporter—you know, somebody who works for a big newspaper—and I'd been giving the subject of graves and ghosts a lot of thought.

The good thing about being a loner like me is that you have plenty of time to mooch around in libraries. According to this book I picked up once, seeing a ghost is not a spooky, Halloween thing, but a paranormal experience. That was the word the author used. *Paranormal.* That, he said, means something operating according to natural laws but beyond those considered normal.

This is how he explained it: We don't know, yet, exactly

what kind of dimension time is. Most of us think of time as a ruler, long and straight, that measures days and years like inches, where you go from point *A* to point *B*.

But maybe time is circular, he said, like a coil, or like glass tumblers, set one inside the other. So possibly things that happened years ago—or that will happen years in the future—are going on now, all around us, in another time warp that we cannot see.

"Sometimes, however," he continued, "and for whatever reason, those glass tumblers rub up against each other. Eras of time collide and intersect and we are allowed glimpses of another dimension."

He finished by saying, "We're still in the Stone Age when it comes to the paranormal, but someday science will solve the space-time relationship and arrive at an explanation for so-called 'ghostly sightings.' Unfortunately, however, I do not think this will occur in our lifetime."

I've read something else about ghosts: That sometimes, when someone is really unhappy, or has a sudden, violent death, the place where it happened holds the echo of the unhappiness or violence afterward, the way the last notes of a violin linger on the air, or the scent of a woman's perfume remains in a room after she's gone.

I remembered the way I'd felt when I visited the guardhouse. Kids my age had been imprisoned in there. Did I feel the echo of their misery? Was that what had spooked me? Or was it the time warp thing, where, in another world, another time, those kids were still there, locked up in the dark?

Our dining room was right under my bedroom. At one point later, during supper, I thought I heard something moving around upstairs in my room.

I stopped eating and said, "Did you hear that?"

"Hear what?" Mom asked.

"That noise up there."

Mom cocked her head and listened. "No," she finally said. "I can't hear anything. What did it sound like?"

"Like someone walking across the floor in my room. There—there it goes again; hear it?"

This time Paul listened, too. "No," he replied, looking puzzled. "I didn't hear anything."

The sound came again. It was a series of dull thumps this time.

"Don't tell me you didn't hear *that!*" I said.

"No, Jenny, I didn't," Mom said. "What about you, Paul?"

"I didn't hear a thing," he said, laying down his napkin and getting up. "But I'll go upstairs and check, if it will make you feel better, Jenny."

When he was gone, Mom said, "You know, darling, old houses make strange noises. It will take us a couple of weeks to get used to the ones this place makes. We've never lived in a house this old before."

Paul wasn't gone long. When he returned he said, "Nothing up there, just as I thought. Old houses make—"

"I know, I know," I said, cutting him off. "They make funny noises. Mom just said the same thing."

"Well, then," Paul said, looking relieved. "I guess we're all in agreement. So what's for dessert, Maureen?"

I didn't say anything more about those noises. They'd stopped, anyway. Maybe it was just the creakings of an old house. But why, then, was I the only one who'd heard them?

The next day, Arnold was all in favor of starting our research—he called it our investigation—right after school.

"We don't want to lose any time," he said. "This caper could take a lot of gumshoeing."

"Put a cork in it, Arnold," I told him. "If you're going to talk like Dick Tracy, I'm going to ask Ms. Cavell to split us up."

He gave me a dirty look but said in a prissy voice, enunciating every word, "As you wish, Miss Muldoon. Obviously, you have the upper hand in this project, since you are its inceptor, as it were."

I was beginning to get the idea that the best way to get along with Arnold was to ignore his dorky behavior.

"Good," I said briskly. "I'm glad you realize who's in charge. Now let's talk about how we're going to go at our project. Ms. Cavell said we could share the research, but we have to put in equal time. Get that, Arnold? I'm going to write about what life must have been like for those kids out there in the cemetery."

"And I intend to find out more about the murder," Arnold said.

"How'd you hear about that murder in the first place?"

"I was hanging out in the basement of the post library. It's really neat down there. They store their old copies of the *Sayersville Weekly Herald* in big old-fashioned cupboards. I found only one account of the murder, though. There must be more."

"I don't get it," I said. "Didn't that article tell the whole story? What more do you need to find out about it?"

"It was pretty sketchy about the details. It only said who the murderer was, the name of the victim, and that the murderer had later been hanged," Arnold explained. "It didn't go into all the gory details of the crime itself."

"That's strange," I said. "You'd think they'd recap the events."

"Yeah," Arnold agreed, "you'd think so, but they didn't. I don't even know for sure what happened. Most of that part of the paper was torn away."

"That hanging must have made headlines for days—weeks, even, in a town the size of Sayersville. It was probably the most exciting event in years. Do you suppose we could get copies of the newspapers for that time period on microfilm?"

"I don't think the library has microfilm going that far back," Arnold replied. "We're going to have to scrounge around in the old cupboards and find those issues the hard way."

"What's this *we* stuff, Arnold? It seems to me those articles only cover your end of the project."

"You're even dumber than you look, Muldoon," he said. "The murder took place the first year the school was in operation. The kids you're so interested in would have been around then. And remember—the murderer was one of the students."

"How awful. Who did he kill—another student?"

"No. He killed the superintendent of the school, a man named Mr. Samuel."

We started our research by going out to the cemetery.

"This is where I got the idea for the project," I said, pushing open the chain-link gate. "It's sad, isn't it, to see all those graves?"

Arnold grunted. I wasn't sure what that indicated. "I've never been in here before," he said, looking around. "I'm not real keen on graveyards."

I whipped out a blue spiral notebook.

"What are you doing, Sherlock?" he asked.

"I thought I'd copy down some of these names—the ones of the kids who died the first year the school was in operation. There were a lot of them. What's interesting is that they came from all over and from different tribes, too. What year did the school open?"

"The first class arrived the summer of 1879," he said. "That's what that big bronze plaque at the entrance to the post says, anyway."

"Here," I said, ripping off a couple of sheets of paper and handing them to him. "Help me copy the names of the kids who died in '79 and '80. And put down everything that's on their headstones, including what tribes they were from."

We moved among the graves, writing down names. The majority of them were very young children, some only seven or eight years old. I wondered if these little ones had died of homesickness. Or was it because they hadn't yet built up a resistance to the white man's diseases?

"This is incredible," I said when we finished. "These kids all knew the murderer. Maybe we can find out what was wrong with him, and what drove him over the brink to such a violent act. You know, Arnold, I think you and I have come up with a really great project."

Arnold waggled his eyebrows at me and leered. "Are you saying you're glad I'm your partner, my dear?"

"No. And don't push it, Spitzer. You're still on probation."

We walked home along the route I'd taken the first day of school, on the road that led past Arnold's house. Arnold was blathering away with his usual I-love-me stuff. It was a hot day, and I hoped he might invite me in for something cold to drink. Actually, I was dying to see the inside of his house. I liked antiques, and I figured a house that looked like Tara on the outside must be full of *Gone with the Wind* stuff inside.

As we approached his house, I heard the same yell or scream or whatever that I'd heard the last time, only now it seemed louder.

I stopped dead in my tracks, but Arnold broke into a run. Grabbing the straps of my backpack, I took off after him.

"What is it, Arnold?" I gasped, thumping along beside him.

"Go away!" he yelled, pulling ahead in a great burst of speed. "I'll take care of this."

I followed him, anyway. His long legs covered the ground faster than mine, and I had a stitch in my side, so by the time I reached his perfectly manicured front lawn, he was bolting up the front steps and into his house. Throwing off my backpack, which landed in a bed of begonias, I ran up on his porch and into the house behind him.

I found myself in a large foyer with polished floors and Oriental carpets scattered artfully about. In the middle of the foyer, under a vast crystal chandelier, was a round mahogany pedestal table. A vase of scarlet roses lay on it, overturned, and the water flowed over the polished wood and dribbled down on the carpet.

A staircase curved down from upstairs, and what I saw on that staircase turned me to stone. I stood there, goggling.

Mom had said that Arnold's mother was a gorgeous red-head. Boy, if only she could see the glamorous Mrs. Spitzer now.

She looked like something out of an Edgar Allan Poe horror story. Her red hair stuck out all around her head like a bush. Her eyes were wild. More than that. They were so bloodshot I was afraid that if she blinked she might bleed to death. Her mascara and eyeliner were smeared, and there were long black trails running down her cheeks. I don't know how long it had been since she'd washed her face, but her makeup was dry and caked, and her lipstick had worked itself up into the small wrinkles around her lips.

She'd stopped shrieking, and now she was crouched on the stairs like an animal, sobbing and moaning. She was wearing a nightgown, even though it was late afternoon, and it was dirty and torn at one shoulder.

"Arnold! Arnold!" she whimpered. "Where have you been? I needed you and I couldn't find you. You're a bad boy, Arnold."

Neither of them saw me frozen there, stunned and staring, in the doorway.

I didn't recognize Arnold's voice when he spoke. It was low and steady and calming. He sounded very grown-up.

"You've been binge-drinking again, haven't you, Mother? I should have guessed when you didn't come down for breakfast."

Then he looked up the staircase and said, "*Oh . . . God!*" He said it slowly, drawing it out, like he was praying for help.

No wonder. I followed his glance and saw empty liquor bottles scattered on the stairs.

"I was trying to throw them out before your father saw them," Mrs. Spitzer said. Tears ran down her cheeks, following the black tracks of the mascara. "But I dropped them and I couldn't pick them up. I've been calling and calling you, Arnold, but you didn't come."

She broke off when she saw me in the doorway, and drew back, cowering and trying to cover her face with her arm. "Oooh!" she cried. "You brought someone home, Arnold. You know you're not supposed to do that when I'm . . . sick."

Arnold turned and gave me a look the likes of which I hope I never see again. Pure hatred blazed from his eyes. I'd never seen anyone that angry before.

"I told you not to follow me, Jenny. I should have known you'd come snooping. Get out of my house! Get out of here right now!"

My knees were wobbling like crazy, but I managed to get them under control.

As I turned to run I saw Arnold—big, strong, smart-alecky Arnold Spitzer, the general's son—burst into tears.

9

Jonah Flying Cloud

Mr. Samuel did not know that Swift Running River and I were with Johnny Little Fox the night the boiler exploded. Many people had come running at the noise. We mixed in with them, and no one noticed that we were there first.

If Mr. Samuel knew we had been stealing potatoes, he would have put us in the guardhouse. That would have been the death of Swift Running River. He told me he would never be put in the guardhouse again. That he would kill himself before he let that happen.

Mr. Samuel had taken away Swift Running River's knife, the one he carried the day of the hair-cutting. But Swift Running River had another. It was longer and sharper than the first, and he kept it hidden beneath his mattress.

When I asked him where he got it, he said, "The boiler blew a hole in the kitchen floor. Many things were thrown about. I found this outside on the grass."

I knew Swift Running River was lying, because he did not look me in the eye when he spoke those words. I was sure he had not found it on the grass. He had probably crept into the kitchen and stolen it when the floor was being repaired.

I thought about that knife often in the days that followed Johnny Little Fox's burial.

What did Swift Running River intend to do with it? I thought maybe he was planning to run away, and needed a weapon. I never thought he would use it for what he did.

Little Fox's death made Swift Running River go a little crazy in the head. He brooded about that night in the boiler room and cursed Mr. Samuel for keeping us on such short rations that we were always hungry.

"Does he mean to starve us to death? Little Fox was so hungry that he gave his life for a potato. A potato!" he said. "He was a fine boy. He would have grown up to be a good man, a leader of our people. And now he is in his grave . . . because of a potato."

Those were his bitterest words, but he said other things, too. He said that he was of an age now to go on his Vision

Quest, but that the white man's government would probably forbid it.

"All our old customs are wrong now," he said, his face black with anger. "Anything we do that is different from the white man is wrong and is not permitted."

We had all learned very quickly to speak the white man's language. We had no choice. We were permitted to speak nothing else. And now that we understood white man talk, and could read somewhat, we were told that we would be sent out every afternoon to work. The plan was that we would study in the morning and work in the afternoon.

Mr. Samuel said this was being done so that we could mix with civilized people and see how they behaved. He seemed proud of himself for thinking up this new way to make us more like white men. One of the older boys told us, though, that the school was getting money for the work we did. This made Swift Running River even angrier than before.

"*We* should be getting that money," he raged. "We're doing the work, aren't we? We could buy food with it. Why should we work so that Mr. Samuel can get rich and fat?"

For our first job, Swift Running River and I were sent to the town livery stable, to clean up after the horses. Neither of us had ever shoveled horse dung before. We were picked for the job because we both were strong in the arms and shoulders.

The man at the livery stable told us to shovel the dung into a cart, which he then drove off and sold to white men for their spring gardens. For some strange reason Wasichus liked horse dung. The stable owner said that many white women even put it in their flower beds.

"Now I *know* all white people are crazy," Swift Running River said as he thrust his shovel into a great, stinking heap. "Who would think that horse dung is civilized? And why should *we* be the ones to shovel it if they love it so much?"

The stable man, who seemed kindly, told us we could have an hour off in the middle of the afternoon. Swift Running River and I decided we would walk around the town. None of us at the school had ever been allowed to wander free among the white people of Sayersville.

We had eaten lunch, such as it was, before we left the school, but now we were hungry again.

We walked down the main street, looking into the store windows. The grocery store had barrels of shiny red apples out front. Swift Running River wanted to take some, but I stopped him.

"Don't do it, no matter how hungry you are," I said. "These people think all Indians are thieves. Do you want to show them they are right?"

"I don't care," he said. "Why should they have these things when we do not?"

"Because these things belong to them," I said, "and we will be punished if we take them. That is their way. They do not share, even with the hungry. Besides," I said, "the man who owns the store is watching us."

A red-faced man frowned at us through the glass. Then, as we moved away, he appeared in his doorway, a broom in his hands. Somehow he made it look like a weapon, as if he would use it to keep us from entering his store.

He was not the only white man looking at us with anger and suspicion. People began to collect in little groups on the wooden sidewalks in front of the stores and out in the street beside their horses.

"The only good injun is a dead injun!" someone said in a loud, coarse voice as we passed, and the others laughed.

"Why do they do this?" I whispered. I did not need to whisper. We were speaking Lakota, and none of these people understood us. But I whispered because the school had made me fearful of being caught speaking my native language. "Do they think we have come to scalp them?"

"We are the first they have seen from the school," Swift Running River replied. "They are afraid of us, and their fear has turned to hate."

"What have we done to make them fear us?"

"Only three summers have passed since our people killed Custer Long Hair and all his men," Swift Running River said. "They have not forgotten. We showed them that we are brave warriors. They think, maybe, that we will go on the warpath again."

"But we are students. We are not warriors," I said.

"I am old enough to be a warrior," he said defiantly. "My father killed his first enemy when he was my age. After that, he was allowed to wear an eagle feather in his hair."

"You cannot be a warrior, Swift Running River. Even if you went back to our people, you could not be a warrior. That day has ended. There are no more Lakota warriors. We belong to the white man now."

Swift Running River spat on the ground, and a woman lifted her skirts and barked a sharp rebuke.

"Oh, yes," he said bitterly, "and now we are supposed to be their animals, like their stinking pigs, to do with as they please. They punish us, they kill us, they take our lands. They have destroyed us, son of Flying Cloud. We must either fight them or be broken and scattered. Can you not see it?"

"Then you should not have come here to the white man's school," I said.

"I had to. It is my fate," he said. "It is my fate to die here, fighting for my people, in this place at the edge of the earth."

Up ahead was a shop that sold baked things. The scent of warm bread floating out through the open doorway was enough to make us weak with longing.

Before the white man came, my people did not know what bread was. They did not know the uses of flour, either. When those who went to live on the reservations were first given sacks of flour as part of their rations, they used the sacks for making shirts, and dumped the flour out upon the ground.

But now, of course, Swift Running River and I had grown used to the white man's flour, and we loved fresh baked bread. Sometimes at dinner we were given soft white rolls, like round loaves of bread, only better. How we looked forward to those rolls! When the cook baked them in his huge black oven, we could smell them all over the schoolyard.

The sign in the window said BAKERY. Below it, behind the glass, were trays and trays of the most wonderful-looking things to eat. There were the white rolls we loved, and also sweet baked things: pale, flaky things dripping with melted *can-hanpi-zizi*—the yellow juice of the wood—that which the Wasichu called "maple sugar." We had never heard of sugar before the white man gave it to us. For some reason, my people developed a great weakness for it, maybe because sugar was new to us, and it tasted so good.

Some of the little sweet things had chopped nuts sprinkled on the sugar. Others were topped with rich cream whipped so thick that it looked like frothy white butter. It was these that made my stomach clench and spasm and the water come to my mouth. Swift Running River stared at them, too, his eyes desperate with hunger.

I moved quickly ahead, putting distance between myself and the bakery. I thought Swift Running River was following me, but when I turned, he was still standing before the window, looking in. His face reminded me of Johnny Little Fox, and the way he had stared at the cooking potatoes the night of his death.

And then Mr. Samuel came out of the bakery.

Mr. Samuel was short and heavy, with a belly like a full moon. In his thick, fat fingers he clutched one of the rolls with the white cream on top. He had already taken a big bite from it. White cream coated his long mustache.

He stopped short when he saw Swift Running River. "Why aren't you working?" he demanded.

"This is our time for rest," Swift Running River answered.

"Rest? You're not getting paid to rest. You're supposed to be working."

Swift Running River had high, sharp cheekbones. The skin over them seemed to grow taut and his eyes narrowed as he stared at Mr. Samuel. "Paid?" he said. "We do not get money for shoveling—" And then he used the white man's word for dung, only it was not a nice word.

"Watch your filthy mouth, boy!" Mr. Samuel said in a loud, angry voice. People gathered around to watch and listen. "Talk to me like that again and I'll have you whipped."

"No, you will not," Swift Running River said, his eyes cold. "Touch me with your leather strap and I will kill you."

A murmur ran over the crowd. Mr. Samuel heard it, and his face turned a dull, dark red. Swift Running River had shamed him in front of his own people. He threw his sweet roll to the ground and began to unfasten his leather belt.

The roll landed cream side down. Swift Running River stared at it. His tongue flicked over his lips. "Johnny Little Fox died for a potato," he said. "I would have died for that."

Mr. Samuel did not answer. He pulled his belt from its loops, wrapping one end around his fat fist. "Kill me, will you? You're a born troublemaker, son. Maybe it's time you learned who's master here."

As quick as a striking snake, he lashed out with his belt. The buckle end struck Swift Running River in the face, just missing his eye and slashing a deep cut on his cheekbone.

From somewhere in the crowd a woman's voice cried out, "Stop! Stop that at once! Leave that boy alone!"

Swift Running River put his hand to his cheek in disbelief. Blood ran out from between his fingers. Mr. Samuel drew his arm back to strike again, but Swift Running River was faster. His knife suddenly appeared in his hand, and in one swift motion, he plunged it deep into Mr. Samuel's breast. Mr. Samuel's eyes opened wide in surprise. Then he made a grunting sound and fell like a stone.

"My gawd!" someone cried. "The injun killed Mr. Samuel!"

Swift Running River made no protest when they tied his hands behind his back and drew the rope down to his ankles, lashing them together, too. I stood at the edge of the crowd. There was nothing I could do.

Swift Running River looked at me over the heads of the

people and called, "Go! Save yourself! This is not your fight." But the gathered Wasichus did not understand him, since he had spoken in Lakota.

"Listen to him," someone cried. "He's calling on his heathen gods!"

Another voice answered, "Well, they can't help him now, but he'll be seeing them soon, that's for dang sure."

"What are you going to do with him?" asked a woman in a wide bonnet. I recognized her voice. She was the one who had called from the crowd.

"Hang him. What else?" answered the first man.

"You can't do that! It's not legal. It's not Christian."

"Injuns aren't citizens, Miz Swenson. They're not Christians, either. It doesn't count when you hang an injun. It's not like they're real people."

I tried to push my way through the crowd to get to Swift Running River, but they were pressed closely together, like wolves at a killing, and would not part before me.

"Stop! Stop!" I yelled. "Let him go."

The woman in the wide bonnet drew me back. She had a gentle face. "There's nothing you can do, son," she said. Tears were in her eyes. "This is a lynch mob. They've all gone crazy. They're after your friend's blood."

She turned to the man beside her. "Don't let them do this, Nathan," she pleaded. "Go get the sheriff."

The leader of the mob heard her and said, "Forget it, Miz Swenson. Sheriff Tate's out of town. We're going to do his business for him and save the county the cost of a trial."

"Good idea, Abner," another man agreed. "We don't need no trial. We all seen this injun kill Mr. Samuel. Right, boys?"

"Right!" came the answering cry. "Let's get on with the

job. Let's take this murdering heathen to the tree and hang him high!"

They put Swift Running River in a wagon and drove him to the edge of town.

They tried to push him down on the wagon seat, but he refused to sit. He stood erect as the wagon moved down the street, swaying slightly but not falling.

I ran alongside. Swift Running River had nothing to say to me now. He did not urge me to leave. His head was high, and he was singing a Lakota death song.

At the edge of the town stood an old tree, its arms leafless and twisted. Was this the tree they had spoken of?

They pulled the wagon under it and lifted Swift Running River, so that he was standing on the wagon seat. The leader of the crowd tied a loop of rope around Swift Running River's neck, knotting it in a way I had never seen before. Then he threw the rest of the rope over a thick branch several times, checking to make sure it held firm, before he jumped down from the wagon.

Swift Running River stood tall and straight on the wagon seat, and he faced death fearlessly.

"I die as a Lakota warrior," he called out in the white man's language. "I go to Wanagi Yata, where the souls of my people live forever in peace and happiness. I am satisfied."

The leader gave a signal, and the wagon driver whipped the horses. The wagon jerked forward. Swift Running River dropped. His weight pulled the rope taut.

But he did not die. His neck did not break. That would have been the quick, merciful thing. Instead, he spun first in one direction, then the other, his face darkening as he strangled slowly.

This is not the death of a warrior, I thought wildly. *He is dying like an animal!*

"Oh, God, have mercy on him!" cried the woman in the bonnet. "Please, God, let him die quickly."

The Wasichu god did not answer her prayers. But I did.

I pushed people roughly aside. They stood like sheep, staring upward. They did not try to stop me. I reached the clearing beneath Swift Running River's feet. Taking hold of them in both hands I pulled down, swinging on them with my full weight.

I felt his neck give.

And then he was dead.

I thought they would hang me for what I did, just as they had Swift Running River. But they did not shout at me or try to catch hold of me.

Their blood lust had been satisfied, and now they were ashamed.

The crowd broke up. No one spoke. No one looked into another's eyes.

Someone touched my arm. It was Mrs. Swenson, the lady in the bonnet. "You did the right thing," she said. Her face was wet with tears. "It was a brave act. God bless you for it."

I walked slowly back to the school and went upstairs to my bed.

I never rose from it again.

I might have, if I could have found an eagle feather to put on Swift Running River's grave.

10

Jenny Muldoon

Arnold didn't come to school the next day. I knew why. He couldn't face me. He was ashamed of his mother. Ashamed that I'd seen her drunk. Ashamed that he'd cried in front of me. I think it was that last one that bothered him the most. It destroyed his cool, macho image.

I thought about him all day, and when school ended, I walked over to his house and rang the doorbell. No one answered. I rang it again. Still no answer. I put my face up close to the glass window in the door. It had little frosted curlicues in the shape of flowers, but I peered through them. Something moved on the stair. Something with red hair.

"Answer the door, Arnold," I called, rapping on the glass. "I see you in there!"

"Go away, Jenny!" was the muffled reply.

"No, I won't. I'm going to stand here and ring your bell until you open up."

The door finally opened, and Arnold stuck his head out. "How many times do I have to tell you to buzz off and leave me alone?"

I planted my foot firmly in the doorway. "Come on out or I'm coming in."

Arnold scowled at me and stepped through the doorway, closing the door softly behind him. "Mom's sleeping," he said. "She sleeps for a couple of days after one of her binges, so she won't be putting on another performance, if that's what you came for."

"Yeah, Arnold, that's what I came for—another scene from *The Fall of the House of Usher.*"

He sat down on the top step and leaned against the railing. "That's one of the reasons I can't stand you. You're such a know-it-all. You have to show off how smart you are. I mean, Edgar Allan Poe. Who reads *him?*"

"You do," I snapped, "or you wouldn't have known what I was talking about." I sat down beside him and wrapped my arms around my knees.

"So why are you here?" he asked, eyeing me suspiciously.

"I must be crazy, but I stopped by to tell you that I'm willing to be your friend."

"Ye gods, Muldoon, why?"

I leaned forward and we were eyeball-to-eyeball. "Because you obviously need a friend, Arnold. Because we're both misfits, you and I—only you're worse off than I am, and I can see that you need a lot of help."

He mulled that one over for a minute. Finally, he said, "You, a misfit? A real snot, maybe. A total fathead, but not a misfit."

"Look," I said. "I don't have time to sit here and listen to your flattery. I'll be blunt. You've got a secret and I know what it is and that's why you're mad at me. But now I'm kind of, like, *involved.* You know, like being a witness at the scene of the crime."

"You're a nutcase, Muldoon. I don't need you. I'm doing just fine without you."

"Sure. I could see you really had things under control yesterday, Arnold."

He looked uncomfortable, so I pressed on. "Does anybody else around here know that your mother's an alcoholic?"

"No," he said. "At least they didn't until you came along."

"How can people *not* know?" I asked.

Arnold sighed. "Okay, if you really have to know, here are the facts. Alcoholics can be pretty cunning about their . . . addiction. Mom's a secret drinker. She drinks all the time, all day long, starting early in the morning. But she knows how to maintain it at a buzz level—you know, where she's snockered but she acts normal. And she drinks vodka, so nobody can smell it on her breath."

"So what happened yesterday?"

"Every now and then something sets her off, and she goes on a binge. I keep her hidden away upstairs when she's like that. That's what I was going to do this time, too, but *you* had to come busting in behind me."

"What about your father?" I asked.

Arnold shook his head. "Dad's big into denial. His career is the most important thing in his life. When Mom's on one of her benders, he tries to pretend that everything's okay. He says she's 'a little under the weather.' That's his way of saying she's whacked-out, falling-down drunk."

"Wow," I said. "And so you're the one who has to take care of her. That's a big load to carry. What alien planet is your father from? Hasn't he ever heard of Alcoholics Anonymous?"

"Are you kidding? He refuses to discuss it. He says if people found out about Mom, the scandal—heaven forbid!—would ruin his career."

"But what's all this doing to *you,* Arnold? You're only thirteen, for Pete's sake."

"I'm okay. I manage. But what about you? How come you think you're a misfit?"

"It's a long story. I'll save it for another time." I stood up and brushed off the seat of my jeans. "I only came over to tell you that . . . well, it's hard to be alone. So if you want to talk to somebody about your mother, or if you need help with her, you can call on me. You know where to find me."

He got up, too. "Uh, Jenny, I . . . I'm glad you came over. Thanks. It's good to have somebody in my corner." He stopped and looked worried. "You won't say anything about this to anybody, will you? I mean, you're the only one who knows."

I held up my hand, like I was taking an oath. "You have my word on it. Cross my heart and hope to die. The one thing I'm good at is keeping secrets."

"Thanks, Jenny. But if you ever squeal on me, you're dead meat."

"I don't squeal, Arnold."

Arnold squinted at me. "Okay. I believe you, even if you are a stuck-up ice princess."

"I wish you'd stop that ice princess stuff," I told him. "I'm no such thing, and you know it."

"That's what I took you for when I first met you," he argued.

"How would you know what I am? You're pretty clueless when it comes to women," I snapped.

He picked at a ragged cuticle. "Yeah, there's that. But don't tell my fan club."

"Oh, shut up," I said, but we were both smiling as I went down the steps.

I didn't tell Mom or Paul anything about Mrs. Spitzer. Naturally. Keeping a secret includes not telling your family.

Yes, I was starting to think of Paul as family. He was a

nice guy, a really nice guy. I'd tried to find something wrong with him in the beginning but couldn't. Paul was like a piece of fine crystal that gives out a clear, true sound every time you plink it with your fingernail, and I'd plinked on him often enough to know.

Mom sure knew how to pick a husband. Both times. I thought of Arnold's father and realized how lucky I was.

Another thing I didn't tell them about was the ghost in my bedroom.

Yes, ghost. Things had livened up since that first night. More movement from that corner. More clunking sounds when I was downstairs that no one else heard. Something was . . . *forming* in that corner.

First of all, let me say that I am not a brave person. When you are afraid of mice, courage obviously is not your strong point. But I wasn't scared of that corner. Maybe it was because I sensed that whatever was over there was sad and harmless and needy. Those were the vibes I was getting, anyway.

And the reason I didn't mention it to Mom and Paul was that they were still on their honeymoon. Well, more or less. Imagine me telling them there was a ghost in my bedroom. That would really bust their balloon. Paul would think he was married to a woman with a loony daughter, and Mom would go bazoo and want to send me to a kiddie shrink.

No. Spare me that, *por favor.*

Sometimes discretion, as the poet says, is the better part of valor.

I sat at my desk and waited.

It was going to happen tonight. I knew that, just as sure

as I was sitting there. I could feel *something* building over there in that corner. For one thing, the patch of cold I had noticed before, which up until now had been present only in the corner, was spreading. It felt like a cold, invisible mist creeping toward me.

Outside, darkness was falling early. The skies had turned black, and the branches of the tree outside my window were beginning to switch back and forth, like an angry cat's tail, in the wind. I remembered my father telling me, long ago, that when the leaves of a tree become inverted, it means a storm is coming.

It didn't take long to arrive. The rain came down, just a timid patter at first, then increasing, followed by the distant sound of thunder. I like storms, as long as they don't get too close. There was lightning, but it, too, was distant. I began counting the seconds—*one thousand one, one thousand two, one thousand three*—between the zags of lightning and the answering thunder. I counted more than four seconds between each sequence. Figuring that if each second indicated a mile's distance between me and the storm, the storm was not close enough for alarm.

Except that there was more electricity—*or something!*—in the air now.

And then I saw him.

It was the weirdest thing. I sat there staring at a ghost. His features were beginning to form in the shadows. He was a total stranger, and yet I felt I knew him. Well, maybe not *knew* him, exactly. I'd never seen him, or a picture of him before, but somehow he seemed familiar to me.

As I watched him continue to materialize, a part of my mind—the part that was not in total shock—wondered if there might be something to this reincarnation stuff that people talk about. I mean, had I known this guy in another life or what?

The storm moved away just as quickly as it had come. The rain quieted. I could faintly hear the TV humming away downstairs in the den. Mom and Paul must be listening to the evening news.

I could see all of the ghost now. He appeared to be about my age, but he was tall and long-legged. He was dressed in some sort of uniform, like you see in ads for military schools—high collar, epaulets, the works—and his hair was cut short, but he was Indian, no doubt about it. It was in his cheekbones and the shape of his eyes and his proud, straight nose.

He stared at me, unsmiling. He seemed sad. His eyes were dark and shadowed.

I stood up and moved slowly, cautiously, toward him. The coldness increased the nearer I got to him. Also, there seemed to be some sort of electrical force field that separated us. I could go only so far and no farther.

"Who . . . who are you?" I finally managed to blurt out.

No reply.

"Can . . . you . . . speak?" I asked in a loud voice, the way you talk to someone with a hearing problem.

His lips moved faintly, but I couldn't hear what he said.

"What?" I said, cupping my hands around my ears. I didn't want to miss a word.

He tried again. This time I heard him. "You are the spirit-ghost," he said. "I have seen you before. Why do you haunt me?"

He spoke English, but very carefully and formally, and

with an accent. No, accent isn't the right word for it. It was more like his words had a different tone and rhythm to them.

"*Me* haunt *you?*" I asked bewilderedly. "What do you mean? *I'm* not the ghost. *You* are."

He seemed perplexed. "I saw you in the guardhouse," he said. "You appeared to me. You were like a pale mist. Something had frightened you."

"The guardhouse?" I asked. Then, remembering, "Oh, so it was *you* in there watching me. No wonder I felt spooked."

"Spooked? I do not know that word," he said. "Does that mean you are not dead?"

"It sure does," I told him firmly. "I am absolutely, totally not dead. I am very much alive. *You're* the dead one."

He began to fade before my eyes. "I saw you in the cemetery." His voice was faint. "You were standing on my grave."

"Your grave? That explains a lot," I said. "I nearly passed out on your grave. Wait—don't go! We have to talk!"

He was little more than a shadow now, but his teeth were white in the darkness and he was smiling a sad little smile. I guess the dictionary word for it would be *rueful.*

"I go, but I cannot go far," he said. "They do not allow it. They keep me prisoner here, in this place at the edge of the earth."

"Who? Who?" I called after him, sounding like an owl. "Who's keeping you prisoner here?"

"The Wasichus. The ones who have stolen my spirit."

The room was silent as the shadows disappeared and the coldness lifted. Even my desk lamp burned brighter now.

Who was he? And who were the Wasichus?

And why had they stolen his spirit?

11

Jonah Flying Cloud

There are many legends about the great Chief Crazy Horse. It is said he believed that the world we live in is nothing but a dreaming time, a pale reflection of the real world. To enter into the "real world," a world that was beautiful and free of pain and fear, he would put himself into a trance. Once, while in such a state, he felt his horse become weightless beneath him. It ran with its hooves not touching the ground. And that, they say, is why he took the name Crazy Horse.

I thought about Crazy Horse and his two worlds now. If he were here, could he explain what was happening to me?

Could he tell me why, when I was alive, the pale-haired girl had been a ghost? And why, now that I was dead, I still saw her, only this time *I* was the ghost?

The last time I saw her when I was alive was here, in this room. It has changed in the years since my death. It is now a place for sleeping, but when this was an Indian school, it had been a place for dying.

This is what happened to me: When the white medicine men saw I was sick, and that I would not recover, they carried me from my bed in the dormitory and laid me in a narrow white cot—over there, against the wall, close to where the pale-haired girl now has her desk.

My cot was not much larger than the box in which they buried Johnny Little Fox. I knew then that I was dying. Many were brought here, but few walked out alive.

That did not matter to me. I did not care if I lived or died.

I was tired. Too tired to rise up and face the bitterness of living in the white man's world. Too sick of heart, even, to try.

As my life slowly ebbed away, I thought of Swift Running River. He was crazy in the head sometimes, and he did a terrible thing in killing Mr. Samuel. Yet he was a human being, made by the Creator, and he deserved a better death than what he'd been given.

As for my part in his hanging—I did only what my father would have done. I have seen my father shoot a wounded horse to put it out of its pain. Surely, a man is worthy of the same pity. Swift Running River wanted to die quickly and with honor, like a warrior. I helped him do that. I had no regrets.

All that had happened, and all I had learned of the white man's world since I left the land of my people stuck like a lump in my throat. It was that terrible, bitter lump that kept me from swallowing the food and medicine that might have saved me.

As my body grew weaker, my mind grew sharper and I realized that I had been wrong all along.

I had thought I would come to this school and learn to read and write in order to save my people. But the school was only another lie, another cruel trick played on us by the Wasichus. The school was a trap, in which they would catch the minds and souls of the children.

When we left the school, our people and our past and who and what we were would be erased from our memories. That was the white men's purpose.

It was simple but clever. They wanted to turn us into dark-skinned Wasichus. Not as good as they were, of course, but good enough to become their servants. And quiet and obedient enough to step aside and let them take what they had wanted from the very beginning—our land.

They would have everything then. Our land. Our bodies. Our minds. Our souls.

And so I died.

But in those last moments, as I lay in my narrow bed, drifting between the world of the living and the world of the dead, I was roused by the sound of sobbing.

There she was—the ghost—the girl I had seen in the guardhouse and in the cemetery. She was sitting beside me, bent over a desk. Her head was on her folded arms, and she was crying as I had never seen anyone cry before.

Was she the spirit-ghost, the foreteller of death that my grandmother had described to me?

No, she was not singing a death song, and she did not seem to know that I was there beside her.

In the loneliness of dying, however, I pretended she had come to be my spirit guide, my *akicita,* the messenger who would lead me over the milky pathway of the stars to beautiful Wanagi Yata, the paradise of my people.

Having her there beside me, weeping, made it easier to let go of the reins of life and slip away . . . away . . .

12

Jenny Muldoon

His grave. I'd been standing on his grave, he said.

The next day was Friday. I could hardly wait to get up and run over to the cemetery before school. I told Mom and Paul I wanted to get an early start on my research project.

Which was true. And which nearly blew them away with excitement.

"Oh, Jenny!" Mom cried enthusiastically, her voice so high-pitched I'm surprised a bunch of dogs didn't appear at the back door. "How wonderful that you're taking such an interest in your schoolwork!"

"I'm glad you're happy with your new school, Jenny," Paul said, looking pleased. I guess he'd been worrying about my social adjustment. I'd even caught him reading a book called *Parenting Today's Teen in a Troubled Society*.

To tell the truth, we were starting to feel a little like a real family. Mother figure, father figure, and teenage daughter. I was beginning to like it. I'd stopped thinking of Paul as an intruder, anyway. He was good to me and he made Mom happy, and that was a start.

The only thing was, I still couldn't call him Dad. I had an idea he wanted me to, but I just couldn't get the word out. So I called him Major Dad or Sir when I was acting smart-alecky, or just plain Paul when I wasn't.

My backpack thumped against my spine as I jogged over to the cemetery.

The grave—it was in the corner, as I recalled. Yes, there it was, right beneath the long, sweeping branch of a pine tree.

Jonah Flying Cloud. How could I have forgotten that name?

I moved closer to the grave, tiptoeing around the other ones, like I might bring *them* to life, too, by stepping on them.

I reread Jonah's tombstone. Yes, just as I remembered. He was thirteen when he died. My age. Imagine dying at thirteen. I wondered what he'd died of. Too bad they didn't put it on the tombstone.

He'd looked sad last night. Why? Or do all ghosts look sad?

Those psychics who are interviewed on TV about paranormal experiences call ghosts "unquiet spirits." Okay. That's a good name for them. So what would make Jonah Flying Cloud unquiet? What had happened to him?

It was hard to believe what he'd said about being held prisoner here. Who were these mysterious Wasichus, and why were they keeping him prisoner? Was such a thing possible?

If only there was somebody I could talk to about this. For one wild, crazy moment I considered telling Arnold. Then I thought—*whoa!* An alcoholic mother is one kind of secret, unpleasant but believable. A ghost in the bedroom is another. Something like that is bigtime unbelievable, too far out to share with anyone.

The branch of the pine tree was beginning to hang over Jonah's tombstone again. I brushed it back. This time when I stood on his grave I didn't feel dizzy or weak or anything. I figured that was a good sign.

The morning sun was rising higher in the eastern sky. Jonah's grave faced the east. I wondered if he had any way of seeing the sun rise in the morning. I hoped so. Where he was coming from last night had seemed so dark and cold.

Some people say that everything happens for a reason. I was here at Fort Sayers because my mother happened to meet and marry an army major. And I had taken on the Indian school project before I knew about the ghost of Jonah Flying Cloud. Coincidence? Maybe. But then how do you explain the fact that he said *I* had haunted *him* when he was alive?

Obviously, there was a weird sort of spirit bond between us. What a scary thought! And now I was supposed to help him, to free him from those Wasichus—whoever they were—who were keeping him prisoner.

Jonah Flying Cloud was depending on me. It was important I do this research properly. I would go to the post library after school and start right in.

Arnold was at school. He was a little quieter than usual, but otherwise he was still the same old obnoxious Arnold. Or at least he tried to be. I could see through him now.

Now that I knew about his mother and father, I could see why he acted so conceited and why he was always bragging about himself in that dippy way. It was just a cover-up, a way of hiding how miserable he was. From what I heard of his answers in class, though, I could tell he was smart—really smart—and I was glad he'd be working on this project with me.

Ms. Cavell hit the room every morning like a tornado, all smiles and enthusiasm. I don't know what she ate for breakfast, but she could have made a fortune advertising it on TV. She had a list of cultural things she wanted us to get involved in that was as long as Rapunzel's hair.

I figured she'd probably gotten straight As in all her teaching courses at college, the way she kept coming up with one project after another designed to rev our engines and make us want to learn. And the funny part was, it worked! Even the poetry thing.

Let me explain about the poetry thing.

"Poetry," Ms. Cavell said in our English lit class, "is the celebration of life. It can be sad, it can be funny, it can be exciting, it can be terrifying. But what it always is, is beautiful."

She looked around the room, her root beer eyes sparkling. "For example, suppose I told you that someone was a pretty girl—a very pretty girl. You'd believe me, right? But what if I said it another way? What if I said: 'She walks in beauty like the night of cloudless climes and starry skies . . .'"

One of the guys in the back of the room whistled.

"See?" Ms. Cavell said. "There's a difference. You can *see* her beauty. You can *feel* the effect of her beauty. Lord Byron wrote that poem. He was a real man of the world and recognized beauty when he saw it."

Arnold raised his hand. "But what if you don't like icky-sticky stuff, Ms. Cavell?"

"So what *do* you like, Arnold?"

"Adventure. You know, something exciting."

"All right, then. Here's an example of an adventure poem. It was written by a poet named Alfred Noyes, and it was about an English highwayman—a robber—who was on the run from the law. Here's how it begins."

She didn't even have to read it from a book. She launched right into it. The woman was amazing.

"'*The wind was a torrent of darkness among the gusty trees,*
The moon was a ghostly galleon tossed upon cloudy seas,
The road was a ribbon of moonlight over the purple moor,
And the highwayman came riding—
Riding—riding—
The highwayman came riding, up to the old inn-door. . . .'"

The room was silent.

"So what happened next, Ms. Cavell?" Arnold finally asked.

"I'll give you a copy of the poem, Arnold," she said. "You can read it for yourself. But class—couldn't you feel the rhythm and the staccato of the horse's hoofbeats in those lines? Isn't the story more effective—and compelling—as a poem?"

Anyway, that was the beginning of Ms. Cavell's getting us hooked on poetry.

I went to the library to learn about the Fort Sayers Indian School, but I got more than I bargained for.

"The Fort Sayers Indian School was only one of many off-reservation boarding schools in the United States," the librarian told me. "They were instituted and run by the federal government for a period of about eighty years, beginning in the late 1800s. So if you want to find out more about the school at Fort Sayers, you ought to acquaint yourself with the overall subject first."

She was really helpful, especially when I told her that it was for a school project. She rummaged around in her shelves and file cabinets and came up with an armload of stuff, some magazine articles and a bunch of books. She even gave me a leather-bound graduate thesis about the school's history.

Everything was marked REFERENCE SECTION, which meant the material was not allowed out of the library, so she took me to a small carpeted reading room with rows of enclosed numbered cubicles. Each cubicle had a desk, a chair, and shelves.

She set my things down in one of the cubicles, noting its number in her log, and said, "This is your study area. You may reserve it for as long as you wish. Just leave everything you are still using on the shelf above the desk when you leave. Don't worry. No one will remove your research material until you let me know that you're finished with it."

I called Mom from the pay phone in the hall to let her know where I was, and settled down to read.

One of the books looked especially interesting. It had lots of really great old pictures and quotes and personal accounts of people who'd been sent to those schools. Skimming through the pages, I could see that it had been a miserable experience for most of them.

I went back and read the introduction to the book. That and the magazine articles pretty much summed up the story of how the Indian off-reservation boarding schools came to be, and what they were like.

Here's the story. It's complicated and involved because it took place over many years, but I've tried to make it as short and simple as I possibly can:

America was moving west, and the settlers needed land. The Indians had been pushed beyond the Mississippi River, and then farther and farther west. They had been cheated and lied to and driven from place to place and massacred. In turn, they attacked the soldiers and settlers who were invading their territories. There were years of bloody warfare, with killings and massacres on both sides.

The white men said the Indians were violent, bloodthirsty killers.

"America has an Indian problem," they said. "Something must be done about it. We must either butcher the savages or civilize them."

They decided to "civilize" them.

Congress declared that the Indians were now wards of the government, and ordered them to live on reservations—tracts of land owned by the federal government. Many of the Indians refused to go. They wanted to stay where they were, and live as they had always lived. However, it was getting harder and harder for them to live off the land as once they had.

Before the Civil War, sixty million buffalo had roamed the plains. Twenty years later, only a few thousand remained. White hunters had slaughtered them for their hides and for the "sport" of killing.

The Plains Indians had always depended on the buffalo for everything—food, clothing, hides for their tipis. Now, with the herds of buffalo disappearing, they were starving and cold and without shelter. They had no choice. They must either live on the reservations or die.

But they found only poverty and misery on the reservations. Greedy officials ran the reservations like prisons, pocketing the money that was supposed to go toward the welfare of the Indians, while the Indians went hungry and died from lack of medical care.

In the meantime, back East, people were growing more and more aware of the terrible things that were being done to the Indians, and they tried to clean up the corruption on the reservations.

"The Indians need to be saved from the white man," they said, "but they also need to be saved from themselves. The Indians are their own worst enemies. To become civilized, they must first be educated. And we must start with the children."

Soon they were coming for the children. . . .

"They meant well," I told Arnold later when he joined me at the library. "They felt they were doing the right thing. They thought everything would be okay if they could only turn the Indians into white people. You know—teach them to think like whites, live like whites, and speak the white man's language. So they took the Indian kids, put them on trains, and shipped them halfway across the country to these government-run boarding schools."

"Was that so bad?" Arnold asked.

"Well, they *did* learn to read and write and speak English," I said. "That was useful, of course, since the country was being run by people who spoke English. But what was wrong was that the schools robbed the kids of everything—their pride, their culture, their language, their beliefs. Everything that was *them*—you know? They were made to feel inferior and worthless and ashamed of who they were and who their parents were."

Arnold smiled a sad, upside-down smile. "I know the feeling."

"And so those kids fell in a crack somewhere," I went on. "They weren't white people, but they weren't exactly Indians anymore, either. Sometimes, when they went home again, their people didn't even accept them. They were treated like outsiders or something."

Arnold was still brooding. I don't think he was listening to me. Finally, he said, "Feeling ashamed of who you are is a terrible thing. Nobody should make another person feel like that. Nobody should have that kind of power."

"Most of those kids were totally miserable here," I continued. "Especially the first arrivals, who didn't know anything about the white man's world. They felt like prisoners.

They were far away from their homes and their families . . ."

My voice trailed away as I thought of what Jonah Flying Cloud had said: *"They keep me prisoner here. . . . The ones who have stolen my spirit."*

What did he mean? I was almost tempted to tell Arnold about him but stopped myself just in time. He might not understand. He might even blab it around school.

Instead, I asked, "Have you ever heard the word 'Wasichu,' Arnold?"

"No," he said. "Why?"

"I saw it used somewhere, but it didn't say what it meant."

"Didn't any of your research books have a glossary of terms?"

"I don't know," I admitted, feeling dumb. "I didn't check to see."

"Well, *duh!*" he said. "Geez, Muldoon, I thought you knew everything."

My face felt hot. "I would have thought of it sooner or later. I was just testing you. *You're* supposed to be the one with all the answers. And by the way," I said, figuring the best defense would be a good offense, "what have you learned about the supposed murder?"

"Nothing," Arnold said. "Absolutely nothing. It's like it never happened. Aside from that little newspaper article, there was nothing. Nada. Zilch. We're going to get a big, fat zero for this history project, Muldoon, if we don't come up with something."

I went back to the books after Arnold left. I couldn't find a glossary of terms in any of them, but the word "Wasichu" was in the index of one, in italics. The very first time it was mentioned, it was identified as meaning "The Sioux name for a white man or woman, or anyone from that culture."

White men were holding Jonah Flying Cloud captive? What did he mean?

Would I see him again tonight, or was last night a one-time event?

I hoped not. Maybe next time I could get him to talk to me and tell me why he was haunting my room.

13

Jonah Flying Cloud

When I was an infant, I was tattooed with the special mark of the Lakota band to which I belonged. The design was pricked into the skin of my wrist with a bone needle, and then charcoal was rubbed in. When it healed, the mark was supposed to last all my life.

This was done so that when I died, the guardian of the starry pathway that leads to Wanagi Yata, the land of the souls, would know who I was and allow me to pass, and I would not wander forever homeless.

It was there, on my arm, when I died, when my spirit left my body, eager to run across the stars to that green place beyond the winds where there is no cold or hunger.

But I found myself here—still here—in this dark place at the edge of the earth.

Alone.

The others who died before me had gone on. There was no one to welcome me to the land of the dead, or to accompany me on my journey. I lingered in the shadow world, waiting for someone to join me, but no one came.

As I waited, I wondered about Swift Running River. What had become of his unhappy spirit?

When I was sick, and knew I was dying, one of the bigger boys came to visit. He told me the Wasichus had buried Swift Running River in a hidden place.

"And then, before they shoveled the earth over him, they covered him with a white powder called 'quicklime,'" he said. "It is a terrible, terrible thing. It burns away the flesh and makes even the bones disappear."

"But without his body, how can he travel the spirit pathway?" I asked fearfully, struggling to sit up in my narrow bed. "Swift Running River died like a Lakota warrior"—I did not add that I had helped him on his way—"and he should go to Wanagi Yata."

The older boy—his name was James Medicine Calf—said, "I do not know what will become of his spirit. I think, though, that the Wakan Tanka, who sees everything and forgives all, knows that Swift Running River had a hot and crazy head. And that Swift Running River believed he was a warrior, fighting an honorable battle, when he killed Mr. Samuel."

"But without his body," I said, tears coming to my eyes, "without the mark of his band—"

Medicine Calf said hurriedly, "I cannot stay long. There are important things I must tell you, and time is short."

He lowered his voice. "I hear that the people of the town are much ashamed of what they did to Swift Running River. What they did was wrong, even for the Wasichus. They are trying to cover up what happened. They are saying that Swift Running River was crazy with the white man's whiskey when he killed Mr. Samuel. And that they gave him a fair trial in their court before they took him to their hanging tree."

"Surely the Great Father in Washington, who rules over the Wasichus, knows they lie and will punish them for what they did," I said.

Medicine Calf shook his head. "I do not think the Great Father is as mighty and all-seeing as the white man says he is. If the people of this town swear that Swift Running River received a fair trial, it will be believed. The Wasichus think all Indians are drunken savages. They have no pity for one who kills a white man."

"And no one, then, has said that Mr. Samuel was beating Swift Running River with his belt? And that Swift Running River felt he must defend himself? What if I—"

"Do you really think they would let your voice be heard? There is a new superintendent now. It is said that he is even worse than Mr. Samuel."

"Why has he not come to see me, then, and ask me questions about what happened?"

"I will talk straight talk to you, Flying Cloud," Medicine Calf said. "You are sick. Sometimes you have been fevered and wandering in your head. The doctor says that you are . . . " He stopped and looked away.

"That I am dying? Yes, I know, Medicine Calf. And my dying will make things easier for the Wasichus. Is that it?"

Medicine Calf nodded. "I think so. You are the only one who would tell the truth about what happened."

"They would not listen to me, anyway, even if I were not dying," I said bitterly, lying back on my pillow and turning my face to the wall. "After all, I am only an Indian."

I could see years and people passing as I watched the living from my shadow world of the dead. Everything seemed dreamlike. Sometimes, I would slumber. At other times, I would rouse and try to gather myself together. When I did that, I would find myself wandering in the places that held the greatest sadness for me: the cemetery, the infirmary, and the guardhouse.

Back and forth I would go between the cemetery and the infirmary, the infirmary and the guardhouse.

The grass grew thick and green over the graves of the children I had known. The foot of Johnny Little Fox's grave always had a small bare patch on one side. Grass would not grow on that spot. I remembered that he liked to sleep with one foot sticking out from beneath the blanket.

They took down the little white wooden fence that surrounded the cemetery and put up another. It was ugly, and made of twisted metal. It saddened me to see the children imprisoned within such an ugly fence. But at least their spirits were free. Mine was not.

There were other changes, too. The school was gone. I wondered why. Soldiers had come and were now living in the places where we had slept and gone to classes. They built great tall buildings of stone in which to work. I did not know what kind of work they did in these places. It was good to see, though, that these men no longer killed Indians.

The blue-coated soldiers I had seen when I was alive were frightening creatures. They rode tall horses and carried rifles with long, glittering knives attached to them. The Wasichu name for those knives was *bayonet,* but we did not use that word, and we called the soldiers who carried them the Long Knives.

When we were naughty, our mothers would make us behave by saying, "If you do that, the Long Knives will get you!"

How I ached to hear my mother's voice again. But I knew that long ago she had gone on to the green paradise with my father and all the people I had loved when I was alive.

The second time I appeared to the pale-haired Wasichu girl, she looked up from her desk and stared at me, her eyes wide. "Jonah!" she said. "You've come back."

"I always come back to this place," I said, and this time she seemed to hear my voice clearly.

"I was hoping you'd be here tonight," she said. "Please don't go. There are so many things I want to ask you."

"I do not know if I can answer them," I told her doubtfully. "I have never spoken to a spirit-ghost before."

She closed her book and stood up. "Jonah," she said, "There's something I think we'd better get straight here. *You're* the ghost. Not me."

"It is very puzzling," I explained. "As I lay dying, I saw you at your desk, right where you are now. You were crying as I have never seen anyone cry before. You were a ghost. A spirit. I thought you had come to be my spirit guide, my *akicita,* who would lead me—my spirit—to the paradise of my people."

She looked at me blankly. "I don't have any idea what you're talking about," she said.

"But you were crying," I replied. "Crying hard. Why?"

"Then it couldn't have been me," she said, raising her chin defiantly. "I never cry. Crying is only for weak, soppy people. I'm not like that."

No, probably she was not. Something about her reminded me of my little sister, Raven. Raven was a very stubborn, strong-minded girl who would rather die than let anyone see her cry.

"All right," I said. "Whatever you say. But when I was alive, I saw a spirit-ghost who looked like you. Naturally, I am confused."

"*You're* confused?" she asked, her voice rising. "What about me? I think . . . no, I *know* that you're a ghost and that you're haunting my bedroom. But now you're saying *I* haunted *you* when you were alive. This whole thing is crazy. It's enough to boggle anybody's mind."

I did not know what *boggle* meant, so I said, "I do not wish to argue with you. You said you wanted to ask me something. What is it?"

She seemed to calm down somewhat. "Well . . . okay," she said. "First of all, is your name really Jonah Flying Cloud?" She looked down, embarrassed. "That was the name on the gravestone. I just wanted to make sure I had the right person."

"Yes," I said. "I am Jonah Flying Cloud."

"You *do* have time to talk, don't you, Jonah?" she asked. "You aren't going to zap out on me like you did the last time, are you?"

"Zap?" I asked. "What does that mean?"

She made a helpless motion with her hands. "I'm sorry. What I mean is, are you going to . . . uh . . . dematerialize? You know, like, disappear? Will you come back again?"

"I told you, I always come back to this place," I said wearily. "Always."

"I don't mean just hanging around, invisible, making cold spots, or thumping on the floor," she said. "I mean, actually showing yourself to me so we can talk."

"I will come back," I said. "That is a promise. And I will try to show myself to you when I do. I seem to be getting better at it."

"Great!" she cried, and then looked anxiously at the closed door to her room. "Uh-oh. We'd better keep it down, or my mother will be up here in a flash, checking on me."

I nodded. I understood what she was trying to say, even though she had an unusual way of expressing it.

"Okay, Jonah," she said, lowering her voice. "What I really want to know is—what are you doing here? I mean, did something happen when you were alive to make you an unquiet spirit?"

"Unquiet spirit? Yes, that is exactly what I am. Unquiet. The why of it is a long story, though, and I am not sure I wish to tell it to a Wasichu."

"I know what Wasichus are," she said. "I looked the word up. You think badly of them. But I'm not one of those people who are keeping you prisoner here."

"How do I know that?" I asked. "Maybe you are lying to me. Maybe you plan to trick me."

The girl made a face and rolled her eyes at me. "Give me a break, Jonah. I don't even know you. Why would I want to trick you or lie to you?"

"Because Wasichus tell lies when they talk to Indians. We say that the white man always speaks with a forked tongue."

"I know what was done to the Indians," she said. "Yes, the white men told them a lot of lies and pulled a lot of dirty tricks. But that was then, and this is now. Besides, I'm not a liar, and I don't go around cheating people."

I narrowed my eyes and looked at her. She seemed to be telling the truth. "What is your name?" I asked.

"Jenny. Jenny Muldoon."

"I think you are honest, Jenny Muldoon, but you are not an easy person to talk to."

"Thank you very much," she snapped. "I appreciate your sharing that with me."

"If I have made you angry, I am sorry," I said.

"Forget it," she said. "Let's not waste time on that. Look, Jonah, I've been reading about the sort of life you led when this place was an Indian school. I know how miserable you must have been. But why do you think you're being held here against your will?"

"Because the Wasichus stole my spirit from me." I could hear my voice grow fainter. My body was beginning to fade. I held out my arm, and already my hand had turned to a gray mist.

"Wait! Wait!" she cried. "Don't go. Why did they steal your spirit?"

"Because . . ." I tried to speak louder but I was drifting away. "Because they stole everything else from me. Everything! Or maybe they are punishing me because I know what they did to Swift Running River after the murder. . . ."

"Murder? You know about the murder?" she called after me, but it was too late. I had gone back into the shadow world and could not return.

14

Jenny Muldoon

My mother heard me calling to Jonah and came hotfooting it up the stairs.

"What's going on in here?" she demanded, flinging open the door. "Are you okay, Jenny?"

"Yes," I said, trying to look wide-eyed and innocent. "Why?"

"Because I heard you yelling about murder, that's why," Mom said sharply. "You were yelling, 'Murder! Murder!' What's a mother to think?"

"Oh, that," I said, faking a laugh. "I was just . . . uh . . . reciting poetry for a class assignment."

"Since when is yelling 'Murder! Murder!' poetry?"

"Since . . . Shakespeare," I said, thinking quickly. "I was doing the Lady Macbeth speech. You know—the famous sleepwalking scene. We're . . . ah . . . going to be studying the play in English lit."

"Lady Macbeth did not yell 'Murder! Murder!' in her famous sleepwalking scene," Mom said. "I ought to know. We did that play my senior year in high school, and I was Lady Macbeth."

"Okay, Mom, I confess," I said, raising my hands, palms upward. "I don't know the speech yet. I was just improvising."

Mom looked doubtful. "I didn't think Lady Macbeth's sleepwalking speech was considered poetry—"

"Blank verse, Mom?" I said hopefully. "Maybe it's blank verse."

Mom still looked doubtful when Paul stuck his head around the door. "What's all this yelling about murder?"

"For Pete's sake," I said. "Can't I have any privacy around here?"

"What a bag of nerves you are, Jenny," Mom said. "Next time you call for help, please don't expect me to come running."

This is why I never—well, hardly ever—tell a lie. It gets too complicated.

I wasn't fibbing about the poetry assignment, though. Ms. Cavell had us reading poetry in our English lit class. She'd set up a shelf and brought in a bunch of poetry books. Some of them were ragged and old and smelled of mildew. She must have hit every yard sale and secondhand bookstore for miles.

"There's something here for everyone," she said, indicating the bookcase with a wave of her hand. "Familiarize yourself with them, because each of you will be required to memorize a poem and recite it in front of the class."

Moans and groans all around.

"You may choose any poem you want," Ms. Cavell went on. "I hope, however, that it will be one that means something special to you."

Dwayne Larson raised his hand. "What if you wanted to do, like, 'Casey at the Bat,' Ms. Cavell? Would that be considered special?"

Ms. Cavell smiled. "Yes, Dwayne. It's humorous, and it's about baseball. It's a fun poem. I'm sure it's special to a lot of people."

Mary Helen Ramos asked timidly, "My mother writes poems. Could I do one of hers? They're not in a book or anything."

"Of course," Ms. Cavell said. "We would all love to hear something your mother has written."

"How soon do we have to do this?" a girl named Sherry Barnes asked.

"You may choose your day," Ms. Cavell replied. "I'll post a sign-up sheet on the bulletin board. And you may each check out a book from the shelves if you wish to get started over the weekend."

Another moan from the class, but Natalie Berenson piped up, "I'm going to do one of the love poems of Lord Byron. I think he looks a lot like Brad Pitt!"

On Saturday morning, Arnold and I met at the library after breakfast.

"Have you found out anything more about the murder?" I asked him.

"I went back to the library basement and looked through those old newspapers again, but the torn one was the only account of the murder and hanging."

"That's strange," I said. "A murder *and* a hanging. Imagine. There simply *had* to be more written about it at the time. It must have been a big deal in Sayersville."

If only I could tell Arnold that the ghost—my ghost!—knew all about that murder and might even give me an eyewitness report.

Providing, of course, that he materialized again in my bedroom!

This whole Jonah-the-ghost thing was just too far out. Maybe I was hallucinating. Even if I wasn't, you can't write a research paper and give a *ghost* as your footnote reference.

"So what are you going to do next?" I asked. "Have you tried looking it up on the Internet?"

"Get real," he said. "There's nothing about it on the Internet. I thought maybe we ought to go into town and hit up the morgue at the *Sayersville Weekly Herald.*"

"Morgue?" I echoed.

"Geez, Muldoon, you're such a numbie. A newspaper morgue is where they keep old newspapers and reference stuff."

"Oh . . . well, do you really think they'll have back copies?"

"If they don't, nobody does."

We stopped off at my house to make sandwiches. Arnold said there was a little park in Sayersville that was a great place for a picnic. Obviously, he was not willing to spring for lunch at the local McDonald's. Hey, big spender!

Mom fluttered over him like there was no tomorrow. She'd never been around military people before, and this rank thing really had her going. I think she believed a general's son was only one step lower than the heir to the throne of England.

Arnold Spitzer? Some heir. Ha-ha!

The *Sayersville Weekly Herald* wasn't much of a newspaper. It was located in a flat-fronted, old-fashioned, ugly building with a big bay window. In fancy gold letters, painted across the window in sort of an arch, was:

THE SAYERSVILLE WEEKLY HERALD
APPLEBY OWNED AND OPERATED SINCE 1878

We pushed the door open and found ourselves in a small dark office with an ancient black safe in one corner and a long counter running along one wall. Behind the counter were shelves piled high with yellowing newspapers. In another corner, an elderly Labrador retriever roused up, eyeballed us briefly, and then plopped back down again.

A plump middle-aged lady came out from behind a curtain. "I'm Miss Appleby, the editor," she said crisply. "What can I do for you?"

"We're working on a school history project, and we need your help, Miss Appleby," Arnold said.

Miss Appleby heaved a little sigh. It was clear she'd been down this road before with school history projects and wasn't looking forward to doing it again.

"So how can I help you?" she asked.

"We'd like to look at some back issues of the paper, if you wouldn't mind."

Miss Appleby sighed again and fumbled around in the ruffles of her blouse. She finally unearthed a pair of reading glasses suspended on a long black cord and slipped them on.

"Our back issues are all bound and shelved. What year are you kids looking for?"

"*Years,* actually," Arnold said. "We're looking for December 1879 and January 1880. The . . . uh . . . occurrence was in early December, but there might be follow-up articles in the January issues."

"Oh, dear," Miss Appleby said wearily. "Not that again."

"What do you mean—*again?*" I asked.

"You're here about the murder and the hanging, aren't you?" she demanded.

"Yes," Arnold said. "Why? Has someone else asked to see those back issues?"

"Yes, indeed, and I'm tired of hauling them out to show to every passing curiosity seeker."

"'Every passing curiosity seeker'?" I echoed. "When was the last time somebody wanted to see those articles?"

Miss Appleby screwed up her eyes. "Let's see. I think it was four or five . . . yes, five years ago. It was right around the time I had my gallbladder operation."

"Five years ago!" I said, my voice rising. "Why, you made it sound like—"

Arnold elbowed me sharply in the ribs. "But has there been anyone here *lately*, Miss Appleby?" he asked patiently.

"Around here, five years ago *is* lately," she snapped.

This time it was Arnold who sighed. I knew what he was thinking. If someone had recently checked into the murder, we could contact him and maybe learn something, but it was probably too late to find him now.

"So how about it, Miss Appleby?" he coaxed. "Would you mind showing those issues just one more time?"

"Well, all right," she said grudgingly. "But just this one time. Those things are heavy. I'm not dragging them out again." She pushed the curtain aside, and I saw a cluttered back room and a set of stairs that led, I figured, to her basement storage shelves. Alias the morgue.

"Oh, by the way," I said, just before she disappeared. "This other person. Who was he, and why was he reading about the murder?"

"It was a she, not a he," Miss Appleby said. "She said she was from some college upstate and was writing a paper about the Indian school. That's all she told me, not that I asked."

I remembered the graduate thesis on the shelf in the library. Was it the one Miss Appleby was talking about? It had looked so boring, like it would be chloroform in print and all bogged down with footnotes.

I wondered what it would say about the murder.

Miss Appleby plunked two big hardbound collections of the *Sayersville Weekly Herald* on the counter in front of us and waddled off. Her dog trailed after her. I noticed he had a big mangy patch in his fur. Just looking at it made me feel itchy.

The entire office looked like it hadn't been cleaned in years. Dust was everywhere. It even smelled dirty. Speaking as a girl who never cleans her room, I know for a fact that it takes a long, long time of non-cleaning to work up to a smell like that.

"What kind of newspaper office *is* this?" I asked in a low voice. "There's nobody working here but Miss Appleby."

Arnold held up the latest issue. It was little more than a newsletter. The main article on the front page was about a wedding. The other stories dealt with the weather and a local auction.

"Miss Appleby's gallbladder operation must have been a front-page headliner," he said.

I carefully opened the heavy leather cover for the bound newspapers of 1879. The spine made an ominous cracking sound, and the first issue fluttered loose.

"Careful," Arnold warned. "Bust up that book and Miss Appleby will be on you like fleas on a hound dog."

"I bet she knows a lot about fleas," I said, scratching. "I think this place is infested." I began to turn the pages. They were yellow and brittle and the edges crumbled under my fingers.

"The paper hasn't changed much in the hundred and twenty-some years since it started, has it?" Arnold asked, peering over my shoulder. "Same format. Same old boring news stories."

"No wonder they couldn't handle a murder and hanging," I said. "What was the date on the paper you found in the library basement?"

"Look for Friday, December the nineteenth. The murder and hanging took place three days before, on a Tuesday. But this is a weekly newspaper, and it only comes out on Fridays."

I turned the pages as carefully as I could. "Here it is, on the front page. Is this the one you read?"

Arnold peered over my shoulder. "Yes. That's it, all right. And there's the missing section."

He started to reach for it, but I pushed his hand away. "Wait a minute," I said. "Let me read the other part first."

The story was mainly about the victim. It said that Mr. Samuel, the superintendent of the Fort Sayers Indian School, was stabbed to death in broad daylight on Main Street, in full view of witnesses. And that his assailant was an Indian student who was drunk and incoherent at the time. And that the assailant's name was Elijah Many Horses.

That wasn't the name Jonah mentioned when he talked about the murder. He'd said something about someone named Swift Running River.

I went back to the newspaper. "It says that Elijah Many Horses was tried immediately, and since there was corroborating testimony by all witnesses as to his guilt, he was summarily executed by hanging. *Summarily,* Arnold?"

"That means soon," he replied.

"I know what *summarily* means," I said. "But how soon was it in this case?"

"Count it up on your fingers," Arnold said. "Elijah killed Mr. Samuel on Tuesday. They hanged him before this paper came out on Friday. Summarily in this case meant pretty darn quick."

"Wait, let me finish. There's more," I said.

"That's the part that was ripped off the library copy of the paper," Arnold said. "Maybe it's something important."

I read it aloud to him: "Members of the town council, several of whom witnessed the murder and subsequently testified at the trial, have assured the citizens of Sayersville that, although swift, the execution was legal and done in accordance with the laws of this county."

Neither of us spoke for a moment. Finally, I said, "Doesn't that sound kind of . . . like . . . *irregular* to you, Arnold?"

"What do you mean?"

"I mean, why did they make a big point of saying that the hanging was legal?"

"Maybe they were supposed to make that sort of statement in those days," Arnold replied.

"I don't know," I said, shaking my head. "It just sounds like there's something strange about that hanging."

"Things were different then," Arnold said. "If somebody committed murder in front of a bunch of witnesses, he got a quickie trial and then they took him out and strung him up. I don't think they fooled around much back then."

"Here," I said, pushing the bound volume for 1880 at him. "See if there's anything in January or February about it. You'd think it would still be a hot news item. I'll finish out the December issues."

Aside from a flowery writeup about Mr. Samuel's funeral in the next issue, and a couple of columns in January about the arrival of the new superintendent, that was it for Sayersville's crime of the century. Nothing about Elijah Many Horses and why he'd murdered Mr. Samuels. No explanation of why a student at the Indian school was drunk in the middle of the day.

"I still think there should have been more written about that murder," I said. "There are usually follow-up articles to a crime that big."

"Yeah," Arnold agreed, "but where else can we look? We've got the basic facts. That should be enough. After all, this is only a class project, Muldoon. We're not going for the Pulitzer Prize."

"There's one more place we can look," I told him.

"Where?" Arnold asked.

"The library. I've got a graduate thesis among my reference stuff. I think that's the paper Miss Appleby was talking about. It might tell us more about the murder."

We had our lunch in the park first, though. We were both hungry, and it was a nice day for a picnic.

Arnold wasn't sure the thesis could help us. "Do you really think it will tell us something we don't already know?"

"I hope so," I said. "I haven't looked at it yet. The writer must have thought the murder was an important part of the school's history or she wouldn't have been checking it out at the newspaper office. And she might have other information on it, too. Those graduate students really have to do a lot of research for their papers."

"Maybe she was a lazy researcher," Arnold said gloomily. "Maybe her paper was no good and she got an F on it."

"Shut up and eat your sandwich," I said. "Haven't you ever heard about the power of positive thinking?"

Arnold pulled up a chair and joined me in my cubicle at the library as I got the research paper down from the shelf and laid it on the little desk.

I opened the cover and flattened the spine with my palm. "Let's try to skim through this thing as fast as we can. Spending the afternoon cooped up in a library with you isn't my idea of a fun time."

"Relax, Muldoon," he said. "I'm not enjoying this any more than you are. Like I keep saying, you're definitely not my type."

"Thank heaven for that," I snapped. "Now let's get to work. This thesis thing better have something worthwhile about that murder-hanging in it."

"Shut up and read," Arnold said. "Haven't you ever heard about the power of positive thinking?"

It did. The thesis, I mean. It did have something about the murder-hanging in it. Something totally incredible.

Arnold and I turned and stared at each other in amazement.

"I can't believe it," I finally said. "All these years, and nobody knew something this terrible happened right here in Sayersville?"

"Not *knew,*" Arnold said. "*Cared.* The worst part of it is that nobody cared."

15

Jonah Flying Cloud

I did not return to the infirmary until late afternoon of the day the white man calls "Saturday."

The room was deserted. I wondered where the pale-haired Wasichu girl was.

Had I told her too much? Perhaps I should not have said what I did about the Wasichus stealing my spirit, or that I knew what the white men had done to Swift Running River. Should I have trusted her? She was, after all, a Wasichu.

And yet she seemed like an honest person. She did not

speak with a crooked tongue. She said things straight out.

I found myself wanting to see her again. It was good to have someone to talk to. I'd been alone a long, long time. Maybe she and I could become friends.

I lingered in my corner, restlessly awaiting her return.

She did not come, so I left.

But I would be back. I always came back.

16

Jenny Muldoon

"A lynching," I said with a shudder, looking down at the research paper on the library desk. "Elijah Many Horses didn't get a fair trial. The people of Sayersville took him out and lynched him."

"No wonder the *Sayersville Weekly Herald* made a point of saying the hanging was legal," Arnold said thoughtfully. "It was a cover-up. One great big cover-up. Everybody in town must have been in on it."

"But that was more than a hundred years ago," I pointed out. "That's a long time. Do you think Miss Appleby knows what really happened? After all, her folks were newspaper people, and the *Sayersville Weekly Herald* was in on the cover-up."

"I doubt it," Arnold replied. "She acted like the whole thing was a great big bore, not something to hide."

"Her great-grandfather might have written that article, Arnold," I said. "Didn't the sign in the window say the newspaper's been in the family since 1878?"

Arnold did a little quick math on his fingers. "Let's see, if she's in her fifties, that means . . . You're right, Muldoon.

Her great-grandfather must have been editor at the time of the murder. So either she wants to protect him, or—"

I finished the sentence for him. "Or else she doesn't know anything about it. I'll bet that's it. After all, it's not the sort of family story you'd pass down to your kids and grandkids. Nobody's going to admit he had anything to do with a lynching."

The librarian came in just then and put her finger to her lips. *Please keep the noise down,* she mouthed at us.

I'm sorry, I mouthed back, and she nodded at us and left.

"So you think the people of Sayersville today don't know anything about what happened?" Arnold whispered.

"Probably not," I whispered back. "It just might be the world's best-kept secret."

"But this woman found out about it, didn't she?" he asked, indicating the thesis. "She says her information came from an old diary she found at the Sayers County Historical Society. Surely, she's not the only one who's read it."

He thought for a moment. "Hey, I know where the Historical Society is. It's right here in Sayersville. It used to be the old town jail."

"Then let's go," I said. "I'd like to see that diary, wouldn't you? Maybe the curators can tell us something about the woman who wrote it."

On the way to the Historical Society, Arnold told me that the lynching reminded him of an old western he'd recently seen on the Classic Movie Channel.

"*Bad Day at Black Rock,*" he said. "That's the name of the movie. What happens is this one-armed war hero comes to a clapped-out old town out West and discovers they're hiding a big secret about somebody they killed. Anyway, he winds up beating the stuffing out of the bad guys."

"With only one arm?"

"That's the great part of the movie. I kept sitting there, waiting for the big fight scene. I knew it was coming. I mean, it was obvious. And then the hero goes into action. Oh, man, the things that guy does with just one arm—"

"Arnold," I said, "I hope you don't plan to beat the stuffing out of some little old ladies at the Sayers County Historical Society."

"Geez, Jenny, you're such a killjoy. That's another thing I don't like about you."

It was easy to see that the Sayers County Historical Society was in a former jail, although its thick stone walls had been painted white and there were little pots of scarlet geraniums instead of bars in the windows.

On the outside, it looked a lot like the guardhouse at Fort Sayers, only bigger, but the inside was laid out differently: The center room was larger, and the cells were in one long corridor behind it, instead of two and two on either side.

The center room was fitted out like an office, with wooden file cabinets and a couple of antique desks. The walls were covered with yellowing maps and some old framed prints and photos that showed Sayersville as it had evolved through the years. A long library table with chairs had been placed under one of the windows, with a stack of little leaflets on it telling about Sayersville's illustrious (maybe) past.

Looking through the double doorway into the cell area, I saw that the cells had floor-to-ceiling shelves, and were being used to store old books and documents.

An aristocratic-looking old lady—fragile and beautifully dressed, with upswept white hair—was shelving books in one of them when we entered. She came out to greet us, smiling. The name tag that was pinned to her dress read MRS. PRESCOTT, CURATOR.

Arnold and I introduced ourselves and immediately launched into our school-project routine, only this time I did the talking.

"We're writing a paper on the history of the Fort Sayers Indian School," I said, "and right now we're doing some background research on the subject."

Mrs. Prescott nodded. "I'll be glad to help you in any way I can. It's gratifying to see that children are still being taught to appreciate local history."

Major difference from crabby old Mrs. Appleby! "Anyway," I said, "we found a research paper—a graduate student's thesis—at the Fort Sayers Library. It's about the Indian school."

Mrs. Prescott's pale-blue eyes narrowed, but I hurried on. "One of the author's references was a diary. An old diary. It was written by a woman named"—I glanced down at my notes—"a woman named Swenson. Gertrude Swenson. The diary is supposed to be in your archives. Do you . . . do you suppose we could see it?"

"The author of the research paper," Mrs. Prescott said. "Her name was Marian Kline, was it not?"

"Yes," Arnold said. "That was her name."

"I'll bring you the diary presently," Mrs. Prescott said, "but first I want to tell you something about it—and about Marian Kline."

She indicated by a wave of her hand that we should all sit down at the library table.

"Marian and I are the only people who have ever read Gertrude Swenson's diary. It was found among the effects of Mrs. Swenson's granddaughter, who died five years ago last month. It was sent to me, along with some other bits of memorabilia. Obviously, the granddaughter had never read the diary, because Mrs. Swenson had sealed it and the seal was still unbroken when it arrived here."

Arnold shifted uneasily. I knew what he was thinking. *Where's she going with this?*

"If you have read Marian's research paper, then you know about the murder and the hanging," Mrs. Prescott went on.

"Yes, we do," I said. "And about the . . . the . . . lynching."

"The *alleged* lynching," she said sharply. "If you go back and reread Marian's thesis, you will see that she herself does not portray the lynching as true fact. She merely quotes from Mrs. Swenson's diary. Isn't that right?"

"Well, yes," Arnold said. "I guess so, but it's the same thing, isn't it?"

"No, it is not," Mrs. Prescott said, her lips forming a straight line. "Marian and I discussed this issue at great length. I asked her not to include Mrs. Swenson's statements in her paper, but she said she must, in the interests of research."

"Wait a minute, Mrs. Prescott," I said incredulously. "Do you mean to say you asked Marian Kline not to put the story of the lynching in her thesis?"

"*Alleged* lynching," she corrected. "Mrs. Swenson was the only person living at that time who claimed that the hanging was illegal. That it was an act of mob violence."

"Well, good for her!" I said hotly. "Maybe everybody else wanted to cover up what they'd done, and she was the only honest, caring one in the bunch."

"Yes, that's always a possibility," agreed Mrs. Prescott.

"But in order to charge someone with a crime, you must have witnesses. There were none here in Sayersville."

"Mrs. Swenson was a witness," Arnold said.

"Only in her diary. Not in a court of law," Mrs. Prescott said. "And soon after the final entry, Mrs. Swenson suffered a nervous breakdown, and spent her last years in a mental institution. Therefore her testimony—if, indeed, she did testify—would be suspect."

"Are you trying to tell us we should just drop all this, Mrs. Prescott?" Arnold asked quietly.

"No, I am not," she replied quickly. "What I am telling you, however, is why I have never made this diary public."

She glanced out the window. The jailhouse was in the town square. It faced Main Street, with its old flat-fronted stores. They'd all been painted and restored, and probably looked the way they had the day of the murder.

It was a beautiful little town. Guidebooks would call it "quaint and picturesque—real Americana."

She followed my gaze. "Yes," she said. "I love this town very much. I grew up here. The people of Sayersville are fine, good people. They don't come any better."

I saw now where she was headed, and what she said next proved it.

"Most of the townsfolk are descended from those who witnessed the murder and the hanging. To tell them their great-grandparents were part of a bloodthirsty lynch mob . . . The incident happened one hundred and twenty-three years ago. These people are not responsible."

Neither Arnold nor I spoke. His face looked pale under his mop of red hair.

Mrs. Prescott clasped her hands over her heart. It was a

melodramatic gesture, but I knew she wasn't faking it. "I think we should let sleeping dogs lie. That's what I told Marian Kline, and that's what I'm telling you."

"I don't agree," Arnold said slowly. "It's never too late to tell the truth."

"But in this case, how do we know what's true and what is not?" Mrs. Prescott persisted. "That's why I haven't made the diary common knowledge. Why should I upset the good people of Sayersville without just cause? Why should I tell them their ancestors brutally lynched an Indian boy when there is no proof it ever happened?"

"You don't have to *tell* them, Mrs. Prescott," Arnold said.

"What do you mean?"

"All you have to do is put the diary out for people to read. Then let them judge for themselves. If they're as good as you say, they'll know how to deal with it."

Mrs. Prescott stared thoughtfully at Arnold. Finally, she said, "You young people always want to pull everything out into the sunlight, don't you? Maybe you're right. Maybe not. I've always thought it best to let the past bury the past in order to keep, as the saying goes, 'peace in our time.'"

She rose from her chair and adjusted her skirt. "I'll bring you the diary now. You have a right to read anything in these archives . . . and to do whatever you think best with the information."

Mrs. Swenson's diary was written in the elegant, flowing penmanship of her day. The ink was faded, but we didn't have any trouble reading it. We flipped through the diary until we got to December 1879. The entry for December 16 read:

Today I witnessed the lynch-murder of a fellow human being. He was only a boy, but he was a redskin. That's what they called him, as if the color of his skin made him less than human and therefore meriting brutality.

The Indian boy—his name was Elijah Many Horses, I have subsequently discovered— was defending himself against an adult twice his weight and girth. Had he been white, a court of law might have proved him justified in his actions. As it was, however, he was not given a chance. The people of this town, maddened with a lust for vengeance, dragged him off and hanged him by his neck until dead.

I do not know what to think about all this. True, we have feared and hated the Indians since General Custer was massacred with all his troops. Even General Sherman has called for their destruction. However, this boy seemed so young and vulnerable.

He died hard. His loyal companion, another Indian boy named Jonah Flying Cloud, stayed with him to the end. I tremble, remembering those final moments.

I did my poor best to stop the proceedings, but it was to no avail. Afterward, I tried to protest it as illegal, but no one would listen. They all pretended it had never happened.

Sometimes, in trying to reconcile myself to the incident, I feel so despondent that I fear for the health of my mind.

The journal ended here.

"Jonah Flying Cloud was at the hanging!" I exclaimed. "Ms. Kline didn't include that part of the entry in her thesis."

"Who's Jonah Flying Cloud?" Arnold asked.

"Well, uh . . . his name's on one of the tombstones in the Indian cemetery. I just think it's . . . interesting that she said one of the students was there at the hanging."

"You have a good memory for names, Jenny."

I closed the diary, my head swimming. *Jonah was there! So that's what he meant when he said he knew what the Wasichus did to Swift Running River.*

"So what are we going to do about what we've just read, Arnold? We can't just forget about it."

"No, how could we?" he asked. "On the other hand, we can't state it as fact, either."

"I see now why Ms. Kline didn't rush out and make a big case for the lynching," I said. "This seems to be the one and only reference to it. If she'd found other information on it, she would have put it in her thesis."

"Then I guess we ought to do our paper like she did hers," Arnold said reluctantly. "You know, report the diary entry—quote it word for word, even—but not give any opinion on it one way or the other."

"You're right," I agreed. "We have to include that diary entry, all of it, in our report. Like you said, we can't argue that it actually happened. Unless, of course, we uncover some new facts about what happened."

"Get real, Jenny," Arnold said. "What new facts? The dead can't talk."

Oh, yes they can, Arnold. And I just might be talking to one of them tonight. I wonder what he'll have to say about all this.

17

Jonah Flying Cloud

Jenny, the pale-haired Wasichu girl, was waiting for me that night when I appeared.

"Jonah!" she said. "We have to talk. I mean, *really* talk. So don't go zapping out on me, okay?"

"Then speak quickly," I told her. "I cannot control my fading. It just happens."

"Okay," she said. "Listen, Jonah, I found out about the murder. I know who got murdered and who did it."

"You found out about Swift Running River?"

She shook her head, puzzled. "No. That wasn't the name. The murderer was a boy named Elijah Many Horses."

"They are the same," I said. "Elijah is the name the Wasichus gave him. They did that, you know. They took our names from us."

"I see," she said. "And this Elijah, or Swift Running River, was your friend?"

"Yes, but I did not think of him as a friend at the time."

"And you were with him when the murder was committed?"

"Yes. How did you find out about that?"

"It doesn't matter," she said, speaking quickly. "But that's not all. Is it true that the people of Sayersville lynched Elijah . . . Swift Running River? Did they really take him out and hang him?"

The room darkened. Was I disappearing?

A distant flash of lightning and a rumble of thunder told me a storm was quickly approaching. The misty gray substance of which I was made began to tingle, as it always did in a thunderstorm.

"Yes," I said bitterly. "I was there when they took Swift Running River to the hanging tree. I saw him die. He died with pride and courage, like a true Lakota warrior."

Another flash of lightning. Another clap of thunder.

Jenny's lips were moving, but I could not hear what she was saying. All I heard was a humming and a crackling in my ears.

"It is Wakinyan, the Winged One," I told her. "When a thunderstorm approaches, you should burn the leaves of the cedar tree. The smell of their smoke is pleasing to him, and he will not strike you with lightning."

This time I heard her reply. She said, "For Pete's sake, Jonah, it's only an electric storm."

"*Electric?*" I held my arms out before me. They were shimmering like haze on a hot summer's day. "This *electric* has the power to do this to me?"

"Jonah!" Jenny Pale Hair gasped, staring at me. "You're starting to disappear again!"

It was true. I was fading.

"Don't go!" she pleaded. "We need to talk. We need to talk about the lynching, Jonah."

I could not answer. Once again the darkness began to gather around me, drawing me back into the world of shadows.

I returned to Jenny Pale Hair later that night. She was glad to see me. She paced the room impatiently as my body formed about me.

"How did you learn about the hanging?" I asked when I was fully visible. "How did you know I was there?"

"A diary," she said. "I read about it in a diary."

When she saw I did not know what that word meant, she

said, "It's a book you write in—where you keep a record of your thoughts and things."

"Whose diary did you read?"

"It belonged to a woman named Mrs. Swenson. She was at the hanging."

"I remember Mrs. Swenson," I said. "She was a good woman. She cried when they hanged Swift Running River."

"Jonah," she said, and her face changed. It grew harder and older looking. "Do you know where they buried Swift Running River?"

"No. He was hanging from the tree when I left. I walked back to the school and went to my bed. I never rose from it again. Someone told me they buried him in a hidden place."

She made a sound of disgust. "It was hidden, all right. Or at least it was in a place where people wouldn't want to go."

I looked at her in puzzlement, and she said, "They dug a pit in the corner of the jail yard and put him there. I saw his grave, if you can call it that. The woman who is in charge showed it to me."

"A woman is in charge of the jail?" I asked. "They have a woman sheriff now?"

"Oh," she said, "I forgot. You haven't been into Sayersville for a long time, have you?"

"Not since that day with Swift Running River. I can only come here. And to the cemetery and the guardhouse."

"Well, the jailhouse isn't really a jailhouse anymore. It's this place where they keep all the historical records. And a nice older lady runs it."

"A nice lady showed you Swift Running River's grave? Why?"

"Actually, I didn't know it was there. That came later.

The reason I went to the old jailhouse was to read the diary. I wanted to find out more about Swift Running River and the day he died." She looked at me closely. "Mrs. Swenson said in her diary that they didn't just hang him. That it was a lynching. Is that true?"

"Lynching? What does that mean?"

"That what they did was illegal. That they took the law into their own hands."

"All I know is that right after he . . . he took his knife to Mr. Samuel, they—the people of Sayersville—put Swift Running River in a wagon, drove him out of town, and hanged him from a tree."

"But was there any kind of trial? Did they first take him to the jailhouse?"

I crossed my arms over my breast. "They took him nowhere but to the tree at the edge of town. There was no trial."

"That's what Mrs. Swenson said. She also said that you stood by him to the end."

"I wanted him to die proudly, like a Lakota warrior. Now, please do not speak to me again about that day, Jenny Pale Hair," I told her. "The memory of it is very painful to me."

She was silent for a moment, and then she said, "I understand. And I'm sorry."

"Tell me about Swift Running River's grave," I said. "Does it have green grass and a white marker, like mine?"

Her eyes flashed. "No, it does not. It's just this little bare patch in the far corner of the jail yard. Well, maybe it isn't the town's fault. Mrs. Prescott says that nothing—not even grass—will grow there."

"Mrs. Prescott?"

"She's the lady I told you about—the one who's in charge of what used to be the old jail. I like flowers, Jonah, and the jail yard is really pretty. It has flowers and bushes and things—except for where Swift Running River is buried." Her eyes flashed again. "But I did something about that."

I smiled. "I thought maybe you would, Jenny Pale Hair."

"There's this hardware store in town that sells plants," she said. "I went there after I left Mrs. Prescott, and I talked to the flower person. He sold me a little tiny rosebush. He called it a Kerria rose. *Kerria japonica* is its fancy name. Anyway, it's very hardy, he said. A real survivor. You can plant it anywhere and it will grow like crazy. It has yellow flowers and the branches stay green in the winter. I thought it might grow on Swift Running River's grave."

"But this Mrs. Prescott lady, will she allow it?"

"Oh, yes! When I brought it back to the jailhouse, she said I made her feel ashamed because she hadn't done something like that herself. So she helped me plant it. I watered it before I left. I'm going to go back and check on it from time to time. Mrs. Prescott promised she'd take good care of it."

"That was a kind thing you did," I said. "Swift Running River would be grateful."

"Would you like me to plant a Kerria rose on your grave, too?" she asked. There were tears in her eyes when she said this.

When I did not answer, she said, "It wouldn't be any trouble, Jonah. I'd be glad to do it."

I was beginning to like Jenny Pale Hair. Trust her, even.

She seemed always to speak from the heart. I did not want to say anything to offend her.

"Thank you," I said carefully. "Your offer is that of a friend. But what I wish most to have on my grave, you cannot get for me."

"What do you mean?" she asked.

"What I wish you would place on my grave is an eagle feather."

"An eagle feather? Why?"

"Because the eagle is sacred. He is the bravest of birds. He is the *akicita*—the messenger—of the sun."

She did not seem to understand, so I explained, "The eagle carries our wishes from earth to the land of the sky. To have an eagle feather on my grave would make my spirit strong. I would feel like a Lakota again. Then, maybe, I could leave this terrible place and go to my people in the green land, Wanagi Yata, over the spirit pathway of stars."

I shook my head sadly. "But it is no use. There are no eagles here in this place at the edge of the earth."

"Have I got this straight?" she asked. "Are you saying you're stuck here, haunting Fort Sayers—and me!—because you need an eagle feather? Is this the usual thing with your people, or do you have . . . uh . . . special needs?"

"The Wasichus at the school stole my spirit. My soul. I cannot join my people until I get it back."

"That is not true!" she cried. "That is definitely, totally not true! No one can steal your soul. Wait a minute—you're doing it again! You're starting to zap out on me!"

As the shadows gathered, I heard her say, "It's not fair! You're always doing this. Come back! Darn you anyway, Jonah Flying Cloud!"

18

Jenny Muldoon

It's a wonder I was able to act even halfway normal what with all the weird stuff that was going on in my life. The worst part was that I couldn't tell anybody a thing about anything.

Like the fact that I was meeting a one-hundred-twenty-three-year-old ghost in my bedroom almost every night.

Or that I'd learned from a reliable source that a lynching had taken place once upon a time in charming little old Sayersville. And that the reliable source was none other than my ghost, who'd been there when it happened.

Or that I needed an eagle feather to lay on the grave of the ghost in order to help free him—maybe!—from the clutches of the evil Wasichus who—he said!—had stolen his spirit and were holding him prisoner.

Or that the glamorous wife of the commanding general of Fort Sayers was an alcoholic who was ruining the life of her son, my (sort of) friend.

I was starting to worry about talking in my sleep at night, it was that bad.

In the meantime, Arnold and I had a history paper to write.

The next day was Sunday, so he and I met at the post library. We spread out our books and papers on a long table in the rear of the reference section.

"I'll write the background stuff on the Indian school system," I said, clicking my pen and pulling a long yellow pad toward me. "I'm going to put it down pretty much the way I explained it to you, Arnold. You know—the settlers moving west, the Indian wars, the reservations—and how all that led to the kids being sent to off-reservation boarding schools to turn them into little imitation white folks."

"Okay," he agreed. "And I'll take the history of the Fort Sayers Indian School. Ms. Kline spelled it all out in her thesis. All I have to do is take the basic facts, condense them, and put them into my own words. I'll quote her as my source, of course."

"And the hanging—I mean, the lynching?" I asked.

"Like we agreed, we'll quote the diary but treat it the way Ms. Kline did—as something mentioned by only one person, an emotionally unstable woman writing in her diary," replied Arnold.

"Okay," I said uncertainly. "That's the way to handle it. I guess."

The truth is, now that I knew what had really happened, I wasn't sure if it *was* the best way to handle it. Maybe the people of Sayersville *should* be told about the terrible thing that happened in their community all those years ago.

And yet how could Arnold and I tell them the lynching had actually happened? All we had was the word of one woman . . . and a ghost.

The only reason I knew that Mrs. Swenson's entry was accurate was because Jonah said so. But that was no help. I couldn't quote him. If I did, people would think I was as bad off mentally as Mrs. Swenson.

Maybe just putting it into our report was enough. If we put it in, we'd have done our duty.

Or would we? What about Swift Running River? Would we have done our duty to him? And just what *was* our duty to him? He was dead, and no matter what we did or said, it wouldn't bring him back.

Maybe Mrs. Prescott was right. The people of Sayersville

today were decent and good. The lynching happened a long, long time ago. They hadn't done it. Someone else had. They weren't responsible.

But it had happened in their town, hadn't it? And it had been done by their great-grandparents. Had the responsibility for the crime been passed down to them, the people of Sayersville, even though they, themselves, were innocent of it?

I wasn't even from Sayersville, but already I felt I needed to do something about what happened to Swift Running River. When something bad is done to another human being, we're all involved in it, I guess.

This thing was starting to drive me crazy. I didn't know what to think, what to do.

But most of all, what bothered me was this: When can people—ordinary people like me—stop feeling responsible for bad things that happened in the past?

I wondered if anyone, anywhere, had the answer to that one.

Maybe Jonah Flying Cloud did. I'd ask him.

19

Jonah Flying Cloud

"So what should I do about Swift Running River's lynching?" Jenny Pale Hair asked me. "Should I tell people the truth, even though I can't prove it?"

"Why do you wish to tell people about the hanging?" I asked.

"Because it happened. Because Swift Running River deserves something for what they did to him."

"How can that help him now, Jenny Pale Hair?"

"Well, shouldn't somebody take the responsibility for his murder? Don't we owe him that much?"

"Yes, but it is too late," I told her.

"Then answer this question," she said. "Why is it too late? When does it become too late to make up for something that happened in the past?"

"I don't know," I replied. "The white men killed our buffalo. Without the buffalo, we went hungry because we had no meat, and cold because we had no hides for clothing and shelter. But there is nothing now the white man can do to make the prairie run black with buffalo, as it did in my grandfather's day, no matter how ashamed they are of the things their ancestors did."

"No, we can't undo what's already been done," she said slowly. "I wish we could. But to just accept what's been done in the past . . . is that right?"

I shrugged. It was a gesture I had learned from her. "To fight the old fights over and over again only makes them go on forever, Jenny. That is not a good thing, either."

"But you still haven't told me what I should do about Swift Running River," she said.

"All right, then, this is what you should do," I said, remembering Swift Running River's face and his angers and his sad, terrible bravery. "Go plant your yellow roses. Water them. Make his grave beautiful. Swift Running River is dead. Let him rest."

"How can he rest," she asked, "with everything that was done to him?"

"He is not a part of that anymore," I told her. "Yes, the Wasichus did a terrible thing to him, but that can't be changed now. Avenging him will not help. It will not change anything."

She was silent for a long time, thinking. Finally, she said, "You're wrong, Jonah. You're giving up too easily."

She took a deep breath and continued. "I'm not talking about avenging him. Or of changing the past. What I'm talking about here is truth—telling the truth about what happened. Not hiding anything. That's what's important. The truth about the past should always be told, no matter what."

"So you tell the truth, and then who will believe you, Jenny Pale Hair?" I asked.

"Nobody, I guess. I'm just a kid, writing a report for school. And you're the only one who knows for sure what really happened. But there's the diary, isn't there? It has the story of the lynching in it. . . ."

She paused for a moment and frowned. "But nobody reads it. Nobody even knows it exists. It was sealed up in a trunk for more than a hundred years, and for the past five it's been stuck away in a back room of the Sayers County Historical Society library."

She seemed angry about that.

"People ought to know about that diary," she said, her eyes flashing. "Arnold—he's my friend—said it should be out where everyone can read it. He's right. Then people can decide whether they want to believe Mrs. Swenson or not. But at least they'd have a chance to read what she says happened all those years ago."

"What about the jailhouse lady who guards the book?" I asked. "Will she agree?"

"I don't know," Jenny Pale Hair said. "I'll have to talk to her."

She was so busy with her thoughts that for the first time

she didn't beg me to stay when I left her. I don't think she even saw me leave.

20

Jenny Muldoon

I called Arnold that night.

"Listen, Arnold," I said, "I've been thinking about that diary, and we have to talk."

"Okay." His voice was flat. He sounded tired.

"I'd like to go and see Mrs. Prescott again, and you've got to come with me."

"Okay," he said again, still in that funny, faraway voice. "Whatever you want."

"What's the matter? You're usually not this agreeable. Are you sick or something?"

He didn't answer, so I said, "Arnold? Are you still there?"

"Stop yelling, Jenny. I'm still here. I was just wondering if I could ask a favor of you."

"Sure. What do you want?"

"Do you remember when you said that if I ever needed help about . . . my mother, I could count on you? Did you really mean that?"

"Of course I meant it. I don't say things I don't mean. So what can I do?"

"There's a bench under the oak tree on your side of the parade field. Could you meet me there in a couple of minutes?"

"Yes. Is it an emergency or something?"

"Sort of. And you're the only one I can talk to about it. I'm leaving the house right now, okay?"

"Okay," I agreed, and hung up.

Mom and Paul were in the living room, reading. They looked up when I passed through.

"I'm going out for a while, Mom," I said. "I won't be long."

"Where are you going?" she asked.

"To meet Arnold. He wants to talk to me about something."

I had their attention now, both of them. Their startled eyes, peering at me over their books, looked like two pairs of pickled onions.

"You're going out in the dead of night to meet Arnold Spitzer?" Mom asked, her voice rising. "Why are you going out in the dead of night to meet Arnold Spitzer?"

"It's not the dead of night, Mom. It's only eight thirty!"

"You haven't answered your mother's question, Jenny," Paul put in quietly. "Why does Arnold need to talk to you?"

"I'm not sure. I think he wants my opinion on something . . . about school, maybe. I don't know." *Ye gods, what did they think we were up to?*

"Where are you meeting him?" Mom asked.

"On that green bench at our edge of the parade field. Look, Mom," I said, "you can watch us from the porch, if it will make you feel any better. Use your binoculars and maybe you can read our lips."

"Do you really think it's necessary to talk to your mother in that tone of voice?" Paul asked.

"I'm sorry, Mom," I said. "You, too, Paul. But why are you both quizzing me like this? Believe me, if I intended to make out with some boy in the dead of night, it wouldn't be Arnold Spitzer!"

"You're being sarcastic again, Jenny," Mom said, blinking rapidly, the way she does when her feelings are hurt. "You ought to be glad that I care about you and am concerned with your safety."

"I'm glad! I'm glad!" I said, doing a little tap step. "Oh, thank you, thank you, Mommy dearest. Now, please may I go? Arnold is waiting for me on the bench, yearning for me and burning with unspeakable desires."

"Teenagers," I heard her tell Paul as I left. "Heaven help us. And this is only the beginning."

Arnold was sitting on the bench, shoulders slumped, his hands on his knees. His face looked pale and shadowy under the streetlight. "Thanks for coming."

"What is it?" I asked. "You look terrible. And what's that funny smell?"

Arnold sniffed at his sleeve. "Smoke. That's what you're smelling."

I sat down on the bench beside him. "So—are you going to tell me what's wrong, or do we have to play Twenty Questions?"

"My mother nearly burned down the house tonight, that's what's wrong," he said. "I don't know how much more of her crazy drinking I can take. She's getting worse, Jenny."

I gasped. "She nearly burned down the house? I didn't hear any fire engines."

Arnold slumped over on the bench, his head in his hands. "Thank God it didn't get that far. But it would have if I hadn't been there."

"Where was your dad?"

"Out, as usual. At some sort of formal awards dinner or something. He's not home yet."

"So who's watching your mother?"

"She's in bed, sleeping it off. When she wakes up tomorrow, she probably won't remember a thing that happened," he said bitterly. "Lucky her!"

"So what happened?"

"I was in the den, watching TV. I thought she was asleep upstairs, but she must have gotten up and wandered down to the kitchen to get something to eat, because suddenly I smelled smoke, and the smoke detector was making this awful racket."

He raised his head and faced me. "I ran into the kitchen, and it was full of black smoke. Mom was standing by the stove in front of a big frying pan full of burning grease. Just standing there, looking at it. I guess she was trying to fry something and . . ."

He shuddered. "Well, anyway, the lid to the pan was sitting right there, so I jammed it on the pan to smother the flames, and switched off the burner. But, oh, God, Jenny . . ."

"What?"

"My mother was on fire."

"What?"

"She was wearing a terry cloth bathrobe, and you know how terry cloth has all those little loops that stick up?"

I nodded.

"Well, little blue flames were running all over those loops. They weren't really burning, exactly, just running all over her bathrobe. I threw her down on the ground, and started rolling her around and beating on those little blue flames with a wadded-up dishtowel."

He put his head in his hands again. "I nearly had a heart attack, trying to beat out those crazy little blue flames. I'm telling you, Jenny, you had to see it to believe it."

"Was your mother screaming or anything?"

"No, she just lay there like a stuffed owl, staring at me with the big eyes, like she didn't have a clue what was happening."

He clenched his fists and thumped the sides of his head, then stopped and looked up at the sky. For a minute there, I was afraid he was going to start howling at the moon like a coyote.

He stood up. "I gotta go. Thanks for listening. I just remembered that the kitchen's a mess. Grease is splattered all over, and the walls are black with soot and—"

I grabbed his arm and pulled him back down on the bench. He was looking kind of nutsy, and it worried me. "Sit down, Arnold," I commanded. "You're not going anywhere."

"But I don't want Dad to see all that when he gets home," he babbled, starting to rise. I pulled him down again.

"Listen to me, Arnold," I said, "and listen good. Why shouldn't your father see all that? Your mother is *his* responsibility, not yours."

Arnold turned and stared at me as if I'd just said the moon was made of green cheese.

"That's right," I said. "It seems to me you've been doing his job all these years. Good old Arnold, the perfect son. You take care of your mother when she's on one of her benders. You hide her from the rest of the world. You play nursemaid. You clean up her messes. I mean, we certainly don't want to inconvenience His Excellency, the general, do we?"

"That's kind of a snotty way of putting it, isn't it?" he asked.

"Not snotty," I said. "Truthful. There's a difference."

Arnold shook his head. "I wish I had your guts, Jenny. To tell you the truth, my father scares me."

I must have looked horrified, because he hastily added, "I don't mean he's abusive. He's never hit me or anything. It's just that, well, he's always been distant and . . . I don't know . . . commanding. Hard to get close to."

"But you're his only child," I said. "You'd think that—"

"He was away a lot when I was little. My mother raised me pretty much by herself most of the time. I guess you could say that Dad and I never really bonded."

"Well," I said, "bonding or no, blood is still thicker than water. And maybe it's time you called him on it."

"What do you mean?"

"Let him see the mess in the kitchen. Tell him what happened with as many scary, gory details as possible. Play up the burning bathrobe thing. Tell him the next time this happens, you might not be around to keep your mother from going up like a torch."

I paused and smiled craftily. "And if he's worried about ruining his career over your mother's drinking, point out what will happen to his career when his wife burns down a house—a treasured historical landmark, yet—that belongs to the U.S. Army."

Arnold laughed. He looked seminormal now. "Jenny, you're bad."

"Well, it ought to get his attention, anyway. Then tell him that if he's afraid somebody will see her at an AA meeting, he can send her to a dry-out clinic. Maybe that's the best thing, since she seems to need around-the-clock care. And it will give you a break."

Arnold sat there, smiling at me funny.

"What's the matter?" I asked.

"Nothing," he said. "I'm just glad you're my friend. I've never met anybody like you before."

Friend. I tried to remember if anyone had ever told me I was their friend. Maybe when I was little, before Dad died, but it was hard to remember that far back.

Almost as if he was reading my mind, Arnold said, "You said once you'd tell me why you think you're a misfit. You were hard to get to know at first. I thought you were bossy and stuck-up. But you're definitely not a misfit. You seem to have it all together."

Should I tell him? Well, why not. I knew his innermost secrets, didn't I? And turnabout's fair play.

So I told him. I told him about Dad and how he died, and how I thought I'd killed him, and how miserable I'd been about it. I even described Dad's root beer eyes, and our "Jenny Kissed Me" poem.

"I thought maybe I'd find that poem in one of those old poetry books Ms. Cavell brought to class," I told him. "It wasn't in any of them, though."

Arnold hadn't uttered a single word while I was telling him my story. Now he said, "Wow, you're deep, you know that? Really, really deep."

I looked toward my house. Sure enough, Mom had appeared on the porch and was hanging over the railing, looking toward us, shading her eyes against the porchlight.

"I have to go, Arnold. But I want you to promise me that you'll have a long talk with your father tonight."

"I will, I promise," he said, holding up his hand like a Boy Scout.

"You're not going to chicken out on me now, are you?" I asked.

"Are you kidding? I don't dare. I'm more scared of you than I am of my father."

Walking home I thought, *I have a friend. A real friend. He's told me his secrets. I've told him mine.*

Two friends, counting Jonah Flying Cloud. And I was worried about both of them. But isn't that what friendship's all about?

21

Jonah Flying Cloud

"Where do you go when you disappear?" Jenny Pale Hair asked. "And how do you decide when to come here? This is the second time tonight you've shown up."

"Being dead is like being in a dream," I said. "Who can control a dream? Sometimes I am at the cemetery. Other times, the guardhouse."

"And here, of course," she said. "Don't you ever go anywhere else?"

"No."

"This place over the pathway of stars, where your people go when they die—what did you call it?"

"Wanagi Yata," I told her. "But it has other names. The Green Place. The Spirit Gathering Place."

"And you want to go there, to join your folks, but you can't, right?"

I nodded.

"And you say that's because the Wasichus—the white men here at the school—stole your spirit, your soul?"

"Yes."

"That's impossible," she said. "Nobody can steal another person's soul. All those other kids who were in school with you—are they still here, too, like you?"

"No," I said. "I am alone."

"Well, then," she said, sitting down at her desk. "That ought to tell you something. So how come they haven't had *their* spirits stolen, too?"

I sighed wearily. If only Jenny Pale Hair did not always ask so many difficult questions. I held my arm up before my eyes. I hoped it was fading, becoming a gray mist, so that I could disappear, but that was not happening.

She frowned. "And what about Swift Running River?" she went on. "If what you say is true, then wouldn't he be here, too? Think about it, Jonah. They stole a lot more from him than they did from you. No, it's got to be something else."

We were speaking in low voices. We always did. She had told me that we must. Her mother, she said, had ears like a hound dog. I did not know what kind of dog a hound dog was, but after that I was careful to always speak to Jenny Pale Hair in a low, quiet voice.

"The guardhouse, the cemetery, and my house are the only places you haunt," she said, tracing the shape of a triangle in the air with one finger. "You keep going from point to point, round and round, over and over again, like a blind homing pigeon."

I did not understand what she meant about the blind pigeon, but kept silent. She seemed to know more about birds and creatures than I did.

"If you can't leave here and go over the stars to your Wanagi Yata, maybe it's your fault," she said.

"It is not my fault," I protested. "How can it be my fault?"

She stood up and moved closer to me in my shadowy corner. "Here's how I figure it: the guardhouse, the cemetery, my room . . . what have they all got in common?"

I did not reply.

"The cemetery is easy," she said. "It's where all those kids are buried—under the ground, where it's dark. The guardhouse is where they used to lock kids up who disobeyed or ran away. I read all about that in a library book. It's such a terrible place, with no windows, and those awful little cells. . . ." She shuddered.

"But this room," I said. "I seem to come back always to this room."

"Jonah," she said gently. "Of course you do. This is where you died. Tell me, when you died, what happened?"

"I awoke," I said, "hoping to be on my way across the Spirit Pathway of stars. Instead, I found myself in a shadow world."

"And what was your first thought?"

"I thought that what I feared most had, indeed, come true. That the Wasichus had stolen my soul."

"And so you've been going to those three places, over and over again, ever since. Right?"

"Yes. I am lost. Lost forever."

"Aha! That's the whole problem, right there," she said. "You aren't *really* lost, Jonah. You just think you are. Those places—the cemetery, the guardhouse, and my room—form a sort of weird triangle. A triangle of misery. You've put yourself in that triangle. And you've talked yourself into believing that somebody's stolen your soul, that you can't leave here, can't break out of the triangle and go to your Wanagi Yata, so you're trapped."

"You are speaking nonsense," I told her.

"No, Jonah, I'm not. I'm speaking from experience. I've been there and done that."

"What?"

"I just recently realized that you can get trapped into something in your own mind," she said. "For years, I told myself that nobody but my mother could ever love me. And you know what? Nobody did. I've discovered that if you believe something is true, you can actually make it happen."

She picked up a book from the bed and opened it. "Listen to this. It's a famous poem called 'Invictus.' That's a Latin word that means 'unconquered.' I memorized it for a class assignment, and it's what started me thinking. Let me read you a few lines from it:

> "'*Out of the night that covers me,*
> *Black as the Pit from pole to pole,*
> *I thank whatever gods may be*
> *For my unconquerable soul.*'

"Did you get that last part, Jonah, about the soul? 'Unconquerable,' the poet said. That means nobody can steal it, either. Okay, here's more:

> "'*It matters not how strait the gate,*
> *How charged with punishments the scroll,*
> *I am the master of my fate:*
> *I am the captain of my soul.*'

"So what do you think?" she asked, looking up. "Isn't it great?"

"I don't know," I said, wrinkling my forehead. "There are some things I do not understand. 'Strait the gate . . . charged with punishments the scroll.'"

She slammed the book closed. "Those things aren't important," she said impatiently, tossing back her long hair. "It's the 'master of my fate and captain of my soul' part that matters."

"It is not as easy as it sounds," I said. "I have been dead for a long time. Maybe it is too late now to learn how to be master of my fate and captain of my soul."

"No, Jonah. It's never too late. Look," she said, "all you have to do is tell yourself that your spirit—your soul—is your own. That nobody can do anything with it or to it but you. Tell yourself that over and over again. Then tell yourself you're going on to that Wanagi Yata place where your friends and relatives are."

I gave what she said much thought. Was she right? Maybe. And yet . . .

"I will try to do as you say, Jenny Pale Hair," I said slowly. "But I think I would have a better chance at reaching the place of spirits if I had an eagle feather on my grave to make me feel strong, like a Lakota again."

"Oh, you and your eagle feather!" she said. "How can I possibly find you an eagle feather? I couldn't even buy one, because people aren't allowed to sell them. It's illegal. Wait a minute. . . ."

She sat on her bed, chewing her thumb and thinking. Finally, she said, "I just had this incredibly great idea, Jonah. Maybe I can't get an eagle feather for your grave, but what if I got something better, more powerful?"

"Nothing is more powerful than an eagle," I said. "He is sacred. He is the bravest of birds. He—"

She waved her hands at me. "I know, I know. You told me that already. What I mean is, what if I got something sort of like an eagle? Something that will give your spirit the strength and power of an eagle?"

"What could do that?" I asked stiffly. "There is no such thing."

"Oh, yes, there is," she said, looking pleased with herself. "And I think I can get it for you. I'm not sure when, though. I'll have to wait for the perfect moment. But I'll get it. Trust me, Jonah. Trust me."

22

Jenny Muldoon

The night Mrs. Spitzer nearly burned down her house was a real turning point for Arnold.

He came to school Monday morning smiling and full of pizzazz. And nice to everybody, too. That was a first.

Pulling me aside before class, he said, "I can't believe it, Jenny. When Dad saw that kitchen, I thought he'd have a stroke."

"Good," I said. "I figured a burned-out kitchen would get his attention."

"I did what you said. I left it a mess—grease and soot everywhere. And when I pointed out what could have happened if I hadn't been there—that Mom could have burned down the house—he turned pale and got the shakes so bad he had to sit down."

"It's about time he realized your mother's drinking is a serious matter."

"Yeah—serious in that it could wreck his career," Arnold said. "That's what means the most to him in all the world. If

Mom had burned down the house—and, yes, that place *is* on the Historic Register—his career would have been over. That's why he was shaking."

He gave me a sad, lopsided grin. "You know, when I saw him sitting at that kitchen table, trembling from head to toe because his career had nearly gone up, literally, in flames, I felt sorry for him. Having him love and admire me suddenly didn't matter anymore. It was the weirdest thing. It was like I was looking at him through brand-new eyes. Instead of "my father the hero," I saw this frightened, clueless old guy with screwed-up values who was doing his best but who could never change. I guess down deep I used to hate him. I don't feel that way anymore. I only hope I don't turn out like him."

"You won't. Don't worry," I told him. "So what's he going to do about your mother's drinking? He *does* plan to do something, doesn't he?"

"You bet. He's going to send her to a dry-out clinic upstate. He says I'm supposed to tell everybody she's off taking care of a sick aunt. Naturally, he'd rather die than tell the truth."

"How long will she be gone?" I asked.

"I don't know. I guess it depends," Arnold said. "That's another thing, Jenny. I grew up thinking my mother was the most beautiful, wonderful woman in the world. But lately I'd started to resent her for what she was doing to herself—and to me—and I didn't like that feeling. Maybe she can't help herself. Maybe Dad drives her to drink. Who knows? But I do know that if she comes out of that clinic and starts drinking again, I'm not going to feel totally responsible for her anymore. Dad's going to have to do his part this time."

"Way to go, Arnold, way to go!"

Arnold took to poetry like a duck, as they say, takes to water. Maybe it wasn't just the poetry. Maybe it was the getting up in front of people and acting like a ham that turned him on.

That morning he treated the class to a couple of poems. He said he was doing it for extra credit, but I knew better. Arnold was a natural born show-off. He liked hotdogging it in front of an audience.

He was good, too. He played those poems for all they were worth. When he recited "The Charge of the Light Brigade," just about every boy in the room—plus a couple of girls—wanted to run out to the nearest recruiting office and enlist.

He followed it with "The Listeners," a spooky ghost poem about a haunted house. I'd read it before and loved it. He did a great job on that one, too, and made me see things I'd missed when I'd read it myself.

When he finished, Ms. Cavell stood up and clapped. "That was simply amazing, Arnold. Amazing! It's obvious you have the makings of an actor. A really fine actor."

She turned to us and said, "Don't you agree, class? Doesn't he have a wonderful stage presence? And the feeling he puts into his recitations! Someday we can all say we knew him when."

Arnold glowed at the praise. Even his red hair seemed to burn brighter.

What with worrying about the ghost of Jonah Flying Cloud, Arnold's problems with his mother, and writing that history paper, I hadn't had time to think about myself and how I was making out in my new school.

Actually, I was making out just fine. The kids in my class were okay. They treated me okay. Better than okay, actually. I was starting to get close to a couple of girls. I liked Mary Helen Ramos. She was shy and quiet, but interesting. And Natalie Berenson was fun. She was sort of the class leader and was always coming up with ideas for stuff we girls could do together.

Maybe Arnold's telling me, right from the start, that I appeared cold and stuck-up helped me, too. I tried to loosen up and act friendlier to my classmates, and it seemed to be making a difference.

For years Mom had been telling me, "To *make* friends, you have to *be* a friend," but I'd never paid any attention. It sounded so sticky and smarmy. Like something you'd embroider on a dishtowel. Besides, Mom has a way of saying the same thing over and over again that sets your teeth on edge and makes you want to argue. But maybe she'd been right all along. I hoped I wouldn't have to admit it to her, though. There would be no living with her if I did.

After school, Arnold and I set out for the Sayers County Historical Society to talk to Mrs. Prescott.

I'd told him what I planned to do, and he agreed.

"Good," he said. "I told her the same thing last time. Maybe if you say it, too, it will sink in. What she's doing is wrong. I'll bet down deep she knows it, but hasn't admitted it to herself yet."

What I planned to do was tell Mrs. Prescott—again—how Arnold and I felt about the diary. That it wasn't right to keep it hidden away the way it was. That the people of Saysersville ought to know about it, and have a chance to read what Mrs. Swenson had written about the lynching.

"Let's go for it, really lay it on her this time," Arnold said. "Why not? It's not like we're asking her to dig up the lynched guy's body and call in the FBI. And by the way, planting that rosebush on his grave was a classy thing to do."

Like I said, Arnold was feeling pretty mellow after his theatrical success.

We were in for a real surprise when we entered the old jailhouse.

Mrs. Prescott was setting up a display on the long library table in front of the window. She looked up when we entered. When she saw who we were, she seemed embarrassed.

"Oh," she said. "It's you."

"I hope we're not coming at a bad time, Mrs. Prescott," I said.

"Not at all," she replied. "It's just that I had a feeling you might return, and I hoped I'd have this finished before you did."

She straightened one of the display items and turned to us. She seemed a little nervous.

"It's always hard, isn't it, to admit you've been wrong about something? But here you are, and I've been caught red-handed. So I might as well say it now. You were right. I was wrong."

Arnold and I exchanged puzzled glances. We waited for her to explain. Instead, she beckoned us over to the table.

"I'm doing an exhibit on the Fort Sayers Indian School," she said. "I've dug out old photos, schoolbooks, student artwork, everything."

She'd done a good job. The items were arranged just right, with the old photos propped up on little easels. I bent closer and looked at the faces that some unknown photographer, more than a century past, had captured on film.

"See? These are the group photos of the very first students, soon after they arrived," Mrs Prescott pointed out. "They're wearing their native attire. And here they are after they've been what the school called 'civilized.' "

It was the eyes in the first set of photos that riveted me, pinned me through, right to the heart—the dark eyes staring into the camera, filled with such pain and fear and bewilderment that I had to turn away.

And then the next group of photos. The same children, but with hair cruelly shorn. The boys in high-necked uniforms. The girls in tight bodices. Again the eyes, the dark eyes. This time they looked into the camera with flat, unreadable expressions. Had they learned at this point to hide their feelings, or had they been robbed, as Jonah claimed, of their spirits, that which made them what they were?

It was only then that I noticed the diary. It sat in the center of the table, the focal point around which the rest of the display items had been grouped.

It was opened to the page about the lynching.

"Mrs. Prescott," I gasped. "Why did you decide to do this?"

"Come," she said. "I'll bring us some iced tea, and we'll talk."

We sat in her small office, holding icy glasses of tea wrapped in paper napkins to keep the beads of frost from wetting our hands.

Mrs. Prescott said, "Do you remember what I said the last time we spoke about letting sleeping dogs lie and burying the past in order to keep, as I said, 'peace in our time'?

And how I said that was what I'd been doing with Mrs. Swenson's diary?"

Arnold and I nodded.

"And then you, Arnold, said I shouldn't keep the diary hidden. That I should put it out for everyone to read."

Arnold blushed, so I spoke up for the two of us. "Yes, we remember, Mrs. Prescott."

"Well, after you left, I started thinking about what you'd said, and what I'd said in return," she continued. "And then I remembered where I got that expression, 'peace in our time.'"

She looked at us to see if we knew what she was talking about. We didn't.

"That was what the prime minister of England said in 1938 to justify his giving in to the demands of a tyrant named Adolf Hitler. He mistakenly thought there would be 'peace in our time' if he gave in, smoothed things over, and pretended the trouble in Europe would go away if ignored. The entire world lived to regret it."

"But Mrs. Prescott—" I began.

"Oh, I know, the situations are completely different. But the basic principle is the same, isn't it? That difficult issues should be faced head on. That it's wrong to sweep them under the rug and go into a state of denial. I thought about that for a long time after you'd left."

She sighed and went on, "I'm not saying the entry in Mrs. Swenson's diary was true fact. I personally believe she was mentally confused when she wrote it. But I also believe, now, that you were right in wanting to bring the diary out of hiding. The people of Sayersville should know it exists and have the opportunity to read it. Then they can draw their own conclusions. Maybe I haven't given them enough credit for being the fine, sensible people they are."

"I don't know what to say, Mrs. Prescott," I told her. "Arnold and I came over here to try and talk you into doing . . . well, what you've already done. You sure made it easy for us."

"Actually, the two of you did a good job of that the other day," she said. "You're quite persuasive, you know."

"The exhibit's wonderful," I said. "What a good idea. It's the perfect way to display the diary."

"Well, the Indian school was an important part of Sayersville's history," said Mrs. Prescott. "And the diary was written during that time."

"So after the exhibit is taken down, then what?" Arnold asked. "What will you do with the diary?"

"I've been doing a lot of thinking about that, and here's what I've come up with," Mrs. Prescott said. "I'd like to know what you think of it."

She set her glass on the desk and leaned toward us, folding her hands on her lap. "In a few months, the National Museum of the American Indian will be opening in Washington, D.C. It's a remarkable undertaking, the first of its kind—a national museum, authorized by Congress, representing more than a thousand Native communities of the Western Hemisphere. Its mission is, among other things, to empower the Indian voice."

She glanced through her office door, toward the display. "Fort Sayers Indian School, for all its good intentions, tried to silence that voice. Maybe too many of us have done that, each in our own way. . . ."

Her voice drifted off for a moment. Then she gave herself a brisk little shake and said, "Anyway, the museum will, of course, deal with the question of the Indian schools of the past century. I think that's where the diary belongs. Let that entry be seen. Let it be a matter of record. If an injustice *was* done, it can never be rectified in a court of law, but at least people—present and future—can decide for themselves if one was, in fact, committed."

Neither Arnold nor I spoke for a few moments. Finally, Arnold broke the silence, "Wow. I like that, Mrs. Prescott. Don't you, Jenny?"

"Yes. Oh, yes," I said breathlessly. "I believe Mrs. Swenson was telling the true story of the hanging. And I think she'd be happy to know that her voice, along with that of Elijah Many Horses, will be finally heard."

Mrs. Prescott leaned back in her chair, relieved. "I'm glad you both feel that way. So that's it, then. That's what we'll do. And by the way," she added, "I'd like a copy of that history paper you two are writing. You've obviously done a thorough job on the research. I'll put it with the display, if you'll allow it."

"No kidding!" Arnold said. "Sure we'll allow it. And by the way, Mrs. Prescott, if you do evening programs or something, I'm always available for readings and recitations."

I rolled my eyes at Mrs. Prescott. She was still smiling when we left.

23

Jonah Flying Cloud

". . . and so that's what Mrs. Prescott plans to do with the diary, Jonah," Jenny Pale Hair said. "I wish it were more."

"No," I told her. "It is enough. As you said, this has given Swift Running River a voice. That's all he ever wanted. To be listened to. To be treated as a person, not an animal."

"Afterward, I went out and looked at his grave," she said. "The Kerria rose is doing well. Mrs. Prescott thinks people will come and visit the grave once they read his story. And I bet they'll visit yours, too, Jonah. Your name is in that diary. Mrs. Swenson said you were a loyal friend to Swift Running River and stayed with him to the end."

"It will be good to hear voices in the cemetery again," I said. "It has been silent for so long."

She looked closer at me. "Jonah," she said, "you look pale."

"But I am a ghost," I reminded her. "Aren't ghosts supposed to be pale?"

"I mean, pale like in nearly transparent," she replied. "It's not like when you're starting to zap out. This is different. I can see your outline, but I can't see things like the buttons on your jacket."

"I feel very tired," I said. "Perhaps that is the reason."

I didn't tell her that strange things had begun happening to me. I'd started seeing her room as the old infirmary. And the cemetery, when I visited it, looked the way it had before I died, with the wooden crosses and the white picket fence, not the ugly metal one.

Jenny Pale Hair still regarded me intently. "You really do look weird. Are you feeling okay?"

I smiled. "Getting sick is something dead people do not worry about. Perhaps a thunderstorm is coming with its—what did you call it?—*electricity*. It seems to do strange things to me."

I lingered awhile longer, listening to her talk. She said she had to recite her poem tomorrow, the one about being the master of her fate and captain of her soul. She said she was nervous about getting up in front of the other students. I told her it was hard to imagine her being frightened of anything.

I did not remind her that she had promised to get something better and more powerful than an eagle feather to put on my grave. I did not wish to embarrass her. Everyone knows there is nothing better or more powerful than an eagle feather.

24

Jenny Muldoon

I did my recitation the next day.

I wanted to get it over with as quickly as possible because the thought of getting up there in front of the class gave me butterflies in the stomach.

I'd wanted the poem to be just right. Something meaningful. I'd finally found this poem called "Invictus," by William Earnest Henley. It had been written a long time ago, and was heavy and used big words, but I liked it because . . . well . . . because it said something to me, something to the private, inner me. And that, Ms. Cavell told us, is what a good poem should do.

What it said to me was that none of us have to be victims. That we were all masters of our own souls. I liked that. I'd been trying to convince Jonah Flying Cloud of that ever since he told me he believed the Wasichus had stolen his.

Jonah was also hung up on this eagle feather thing. He needed an eagle feather, he said, to give him the strength to go to his Wanagi Yata place.

I had no idea where to get an eagle feather. But then I got a really great idea. At least, it seemed great at the time. So I said, "What if I got something sort of like an eagle? Something that will give your spirit the strength and power of an eagle?"

"There is no such thing," he said.

"Oh, yes, there is," I told him. "And I think I can get it for you. Trust me, Jonah. Trust me."

Me and my big mouth. Now I had to come through with the eagle feather substitute or die trying.

Actually, I exaggerated. I wouldn't have to die trying, but I would have to face Paul and ask him to do me a big favor. I wasn't quite sure how to handle it. So I figured, what the heck, I'll just tell him the truth. As much of it as I dared tell, anyway.

"Paul," I said, "if I asked a favor of you, would you do it?"

"Of course I would, Jenny. You ought to know that."

"Well, this means you giving me something. Something that means a lot to you."

"Like what?"

"Do you remember the day you showed me your medals and military ribbons and patches?"

"Yes. Why? Do you want me to give you one of them?"

"Well, yes. But I can't return it. And I can't tell you why I need it."

"Which one do you want?" he asked.

"If you let me see them, I'll point it out to you," I told him.

Paul went to the back of the house, to the little den that had his desk and his bookcases and military things. He returned carrying a large scuffed jewelry case. "Was it in here?" he asked.

"Yes," I said. "That's where I saw it."

He opened the case and held it out to me. His medals were in one section, his ribbons in another. And in the center were his military patches.

Military patches were something I didn't know anything about until Mom married Paul. It seems that many military units have unique cloth patches to identify them. Sometimes they have the number of the unit embroidered on it, like the big red "1" that means the First Division. Sometimes they have symbols on them, like the black horse head, which is a famous old cavalry unit. Paul had several patches, since he'd been in the army for more than twenty years and had done a lot of things.

I found the one I was looking for and pulled it out. I was very nervous.

"This is the one I'd like, if it's okay with you."

I remembered Paul telling me that this old patch was special, because a colonel Paul admired very much had given it to him. I saw the look on his face as I showed him the patch, and I knew it would be a tremendous sacrifice for him to give it to me.

"It's my 101st Airborne Division patch," he said in a quiet voice. "Colonel Bartlett, my old commanding officer, gave it to me when I joined his unit. He'd worn it when he jumped into Normandy in 1944. It was on his sleeve all through the Battle of the Bulge. I felt privileged to wear it."

"Oh, Paul," I said, putting the patch back into the case. "I can't do this. I can't ask this of you. It means too much to you."

"But how much does it mean to *you?*" he asked. "It must

mean a lot or you wouldn't have asked me for it in the first place."

"Yes, it does," I said. "It's really important to me."

"I got this long ago, back when I was young and foolish and used to parachute out of airplanes. I always said it brought me good luck," Paul said, half to himself.

"Please," I said. "You're making me feel awful. I never should have asked you for this. I wouldn't have, except that . . ."

He cleared his throat, like he was feeling kind of emotional and was embarrassed about it.

"Look, Paul," I said. "I can't even explain to you why I need this patch. Maybe someday I'll be able to tell you about it, but then again, maybe I won't. And remember, I can't return it, either."

"It's okay, Jenny," he said, putting it in my hand. "Here. Take it. I don't need that kind of luck anymore. I'm too old now—and too sensible—to jump out of airplanes. Besides, your mother and you have brought me all the good luck I need from here on out."

I looked into his kind, steady gray eyes, and felt my chin wobble a little. I had to blink fast to keep from getting teary.

There were a lot of things I wanted to tell him. Like how glad I was he married Mom. And how grateful I was that he liked me, in spite of the snotty, rotten way I'd treated him at first. But if I did, I might start bawling and embarrass us both.

Instead, I stood on tiptoe and gave him a quick kiss on the cheek. It was the first time I'd ever done that. "Thanks . . . Dad," I said.

This time it was *his* chin that wobbled.

The sun was far in the west when I entered the cemetery. It cast a long shadow across Jonah's grave.

I knelt beside his grave and took one last look at Paul's patch. It was black and shaped like a shield. The word AIRBORNE was embroidered in gold across the top arch of the shield. On the face of the shield was an American eagle in profile—white, with a gold beak. Its mouth was open, and its red tongue showed. It was screaming. A screaming eagle.

That's what the men of the 101st Airborne are called. Screaming Eagles. Paul told me that the first time I saw the patch. The 101st is an elite unit, composed of brave fighting men. They'd fought in World War II and Vietnam and in the Gulf War.

I looked around for Jonah. I couldn't see him, but somehow I felt his presence. So I talked aloud to him as I pushed the patch down—deep down—into the narrow space between the base of the headstone and the grave itself.

"I know you can hear me, Jonah," I said. "And I did what I promised. I brought you your eagle. It's not a feather, like you wanted, but I think it's even better."

The graveyard fell eerily silent. Even the crickets stopped chirping, as if they, too, were listening.

"It's a patch—a picture on cloth—of a screaming eagle. The soldiers who wear this patch are called Screaming Eagles. They are very brave, Jonah, just like your Lakota warriors. They jump down out of the sky from airplanes—big, metal birds—to do battle. What keeps them from falling to their deaths are parachutes. Parachutes are like wide white wings. White eagle wings."

I raised my head and listened. Still no sound in the cemetery. So I continued: "What these men do is very dangerous. But they are willing to give their lives for what they believe is right. Some of them have even won the Congressional Medal of Honor. That's the very highest award you can get for bravery in this country."

Still that feeling of someone holding his breath, listening.

"You told me the eagle is the messenger of the sun. These Screaming Eagles drop down out of the sun, too. They will make your spirit strong. As strong as an eagle would."

I stood up and took a paper from my pocket. It was something I'd copied from the Bible. Unfolding it, I said, "I don't know what kind of a funeral you got, Jonah, but here's something they probably didn't read over your grave. It's about eagles. And when I talk about the Lord, I want you to know I'm talking about your Wakan Tanka, because to me they sound like they're the very same."

I cleared my throat and began to read. "'They that wait upon the Lord shall renew their strength. They shall mount up with wings as eagles. They shall run, and not be weary. And they shall walk, and not faint.'"

I shifted from one foot to the other, not knowing what to say next. Finally, I said, "You said an eagle feather would make you strong and set you free. Well, I hope this does the trick for you. A bit of me is in that patch, too, because I got it from my . . . my father. He's a warrior, and he wore this when he dropped out of the sky like an eagle.

"So maybe you can go off now to your Wanagi Yata. And if you do, I want you to know one thing. I'm going to miss you. I mean, like, miss you a lot. I know I'll probably miss you more than you will me, because I'm the one who'll be left behind. But I'm glad we were friends, Jonah Flying Cloud, even for a short time."

In the grass, a chorus of crickets began to chirp once more.

I went home, the way I always went home from the cemetery, past Arnold's house.

"Hey, Jenny! Wait up!" he shouted, bolting down the front steps. "I've got something for you."

I stopped. "What is it?"

He was out of breath when he caught up with me. "I found that poem. That poem your father used to recite to you."

"You did? Where'd you find it?"

"I went to the library in town. Their books go back to Noah's ark. And I found your poem. Here. Take it. I copied it on their machine."

"You went all the way into town just to find me that poem?"

He blushed and looked down. "Nothing personal, I only wanted to see what you were talking about."

"That's just about the nicest thing anybody ever did for me." I pulled his head down and kissed him on the cheek. "Thank you. Thank you, Arnold."

For once, the great Arnold Spitzer was speechless. His jaw was still sagging when I turned the corner and headed for home.

I waited until after supper to read the "Jenny Kissed Me" poem. I wanted to be alone when I did.

After I'd done the dishes, I told Mom I had a lot of homework to do, and went upstairs to my room. My hands were trembling and clammy as I unfolded the paper Arnold had given me. I sat down at my desk and smoothed it flat with my hand.

I didn't recognize the title. "Rondeau." I always thought it was called "Jenny Kissed Me."

The author's name was Leigh Hunt, and the date on the poem was 1838. Wow. To think that the poem had lasted all those years. And that way back then, somebody had loved a girl named Jenny enough to write a poem about her.

Here's the poem:

Jenny kissed me when we met,
Jumping from the chair she sat in;
Time, you thief, who love to get
Sweets into your list, put that in:
Say I'm weary, say I'm sad,
Say that health and wealth have missed me,
Say I'm growing old, but add,
Jenny kissed me.

It was the poem, the very same poem that Daddy always recited to me. I thought of what life had been like then. Dad and his root beer eyes. How he'd picked me up and swung me in his arms.

And then I started crying. I put my head down on the desk and cried like I've never cried before.

I cried for my father, because I loved him and still missed him, even now. I cried for Arnold and his poor alcoholic mother and his jerky father. And for Jonah Flying Cloud, who'd been longing for more than a hundred years to join his people in Wanagi Yata. And for Swift Running River, who'd come to such a terrible end.

I cried for all those little kids in that Indian cemetery, who'd died so young and half a continent away from their loved ones.

I cried and cried.

Until I felt the cold.

I raised my head and looked around.

It wasn't my bedroom anymore. It was an infirmary. And over to my left, Jonah Flying Cloud was dying in a narrow hospital bed.

I knew he was dying, because he looked thin and weak and his eyes were closed.

But he must have felt me looking at him, because he opened his eyes and said, with a joyful smile that nearly tore my heart apart, "Jenny! Jenny Pale Hair! This time I know who you are!"

25

Jonah Flying Cloud

I was dying. Again.

I remembered the other time. And the Wasichu girl who had cried. Once again her weeping roused me from my dreaming.

"Jenny! Jenny Pale Hair!" I cried. "This time I know who you are!"

"Oh, Jonah!" She jumped up from her chair and came to me, dropping to her knees beside my bed. She reached out and took my hand in hers, and then looked down, startled.

"I can feel your hand," she said. "I never could touch you

before. You were just mist. What happened? Am I in your time, or are you in mine?"

"I think our times have come together, but only for a little while," I told her. "Your hand is warm. It is a comfort to me."

"The eagle, Jonah. Were you there when I put it on your grave?"

"Yes, I was watching. It was a wonderful, kind thing you did for me, and I thank you for it."

I closed my eyes again, because it was hard to keep them open and I was very tired. But I had things I must say to her, so I opened them again and said, "I saw you the last time, too. The other time I died. I pretended you had come to be my spirit guide, my *akicita,* who would lead me to Wanagi Yata."

"But you didn't get there," she said. "Jonah, you have to make it this time. I wish I *could* lead you to your Wanagi Yata. What can I do to make it happen?"

"You can talk to me, Jenny Pale Hair," I said, my voice low and weak. "Tell me about my spirit, and how no one can take it from me."

She put her face closer to mine and took a firmer grip on my hand. "All right. Listen to me, Jonah. Your soul—your spirit—belongs only to you. No one can harm it. No one can take it away from you. No matter what someone does to your body, they can't touch your spirit."

She took a deep breath and continued in a low, intense voice. "You can choose—right now—where your spirit will go. If you want to go to Wanagi Yata, then choose to go there. Tell yourself that when you awaken, you will be in the Green Place with your people. Say it, Jonah, say it!"

"I choose to go to Wanagi Yata," I repeated. "When I awaken, I will be in the Green Place with my people."

"And you *will* be there," she said. "You will. I know it. That's why you've been given a second chance. That's why I'm here. I was your ghost, and you've been mine. For some crazy reason, we were fated to know each other, even though we lived in different times."

"You have been a good friend," I said. "I'm glad it was you who was sent to help me. But I can speak no more. I think the time has come for me to go."

A dark mist began to swirl about me. I was disappearing, back into my own time. Faintly, and across the gathering years, I heard the voice of Jenny Pale Hair calling my name.

When I opened my eyes, I was bathed in white light.

The walls of the infirmary had disappeared. Ahead lay the milky pathway of stars that would take me to my people.

I remembered the words Jenny read over my grave, and I rose up as if on eagles' wings. I walked across the stars and did not faint. I ran and was not weary.

At the other end of the starry pathway lay a green and shining land where bright sunflowers bloomed. Herds of buffalo moved on the distant prairie. Blue lakes sparkled in the sunlight. Birds wheeled and sang in the sky.

My family was there to meet me. My mother and father. My little sister, Raven. My grandparents. With them were Swift Running River and Johnny Little Fox.

They all laughed joyfully as I ran toward them.

26

Jenny Muldoon

Arnold and I got an A+ on our history paper. Ms. Cavell said it was so well done, and of such importance to all of us, that Arnold and I should read it aloud to the class.

The class discussion that followed went on for a long time.

In our report, Arnold and I had quoted the entry in Mrs. Swenson's diary about the lynching. We wrote it as we'd agreed—stating that it might or might not be true. Only I knew the truth of it, but had to pretend ignorance.

Some of the kids believed Mrs. Swenson. Some didn't. But everyone wanted to go to the old jailhouse and put flowers on Swift Running River's grave. They called him by his Wasichu name, Elijah Many Horses. I had to be careful when I spoke of him. No one else knew his true name.

They were also moved by what Mrs. Swenson had said of Jonah Flying Cloud, how he'd been loyal to Elijah and stayed with him to the end.

As Mary Helen Ramos said, "Whether Elijah Many Horses was lynched or legally hanged, it was a hard way to die. It was good he had a friend beside him when he did."

Mrs. Prescott was surprised at how the people of Sayersville reacted to Mrs. Swenson's diary.

"I thought they'd be angry or torn apart by that entry," she told Arnold and me. "But it's been just the opposite. Everyone who reads it comes away quiet and thoughtful. Some even have tears in their eyes."

"Maybe those people know more about that hanging than anybody let on," I suggested.

"That's possible," Mrs. Prescott admitted. "Family stories do have a way of leaking down through the generations, although more as vague little rumors than actual fact."

"I guess we'll never find out what really happened,"

Arnold said. "But Mrs. Swenson's words have been heard. That's the important thing."

"Yes," agreed Mrs. Prescott. "And I'm glad I was a part of it."

Mrs. Prescott decided to hold an evening reception at the old jailhouse to further publicize the display. Somehow she'd gotten more items for the exhibit: old school uniforms, a setting of china from the dining hall, a pair of buckskins one of the boys had worn when he arrived—things like that.

"People had them in their attics," she said. "I don't know how they got them or why they still had them, but the display and that diary have caused an amazing renewal of interest in the Indian school."

She even asked Arnold and me to read our history paper to the group.

"Hey, Muldoon," he said. "Maybe we ought to get paid for doing this." But he looked pretty pumped up about being asked.

So we read our paper again. And again people listened, only it was a room full of grownups this time.

This is how the report ended. Arnold read that part, and put a lot of emotion into it.

"Indian schools like the one at Fort Sayers robbed our country. They robbed all of us, because in breaking the Indian children down and then re-creating them in the white man's image, we were denied their uniqueness. We were denied the beauty of a bright and glorious thread in the fabric of our country."

General Spitzer attended the reception. Afterward he came up to Arnold and told him he was proud of him. I was across the room talking to somebody else when he did it, but Arnold told me about it later.

"I couldn't believe it, Jenny. I think he really meant it. This is the first time he's ever said anything like that to me."

"People change, I guess," I said. "Mellow out. You sure have. I have, too. It can happen even to the worst of us."

Mom and Paul were also there that night. Mom said, "Jenny, I thought you were only writing a history paper. I had no idea you were involved in more than just a class assignment. The diary business, and the rosebush out there on that grave—everything." She made a sweeping gesture that nearly knocked the hat off a little old lady sipping punch.

"So why didn't you tell Paul and me about all this?" she asked.

"There's a lot I haven't told you," I said. "A lot. And I'll tell you everything someday. But not yet. Not now."

"It's okay, Jenny," Paul said, patting me awkwardly on the shoulder. "Don't tell us until you're ready. I have a feeling that what you say will be well worth the wait."

I walked over to the cemetery after school the next day and went to Jonah's grave.

"I know you aren't here anymore, Jonah," I said, "but just in case, somehow, you can still hear me, I wanted you to know that the yellow Kerria rosebush on Swift Running River's grave is doing well. It's spread and put up new shoots where nothing has ever grown before."

I looked around the cemetery. Autumn had come, and the grass was beginning to turn. Soon it would be brown and dead, and the snows would fall, blanketing the little graves. But then spring would come, as it always does, and the grass would grow green again.

"Did I tell you, Jonah, that the Kerria rose blooms in the early spring? I'm going to get another one, and plant it over there, in the corner. When it grows, it will touch your grave. And I like the idea of it blooming to show when winter is over, don't you?"

Overhead a flock of Canada geese honked as they made their way south. The sun was beginning to go down. It grew dark early these days. I pulled my sweater closer about me.

"I probably ought to go. If anybody saw me standing here, talking to myself, they'd think I was crazy. But . . . well, the truth is, I miss you, Jonah. I miss you a lot."

I bent over and checked where I'd pushed the Screaming Eagle patch down between the headstone and the earth. It was okay. I'd pushed it down far enough so it wouldn't get rained on or snowed on when winter came. It was safe, almost as if it lay close against Jonah's heart.

"There's something else I wanted to tell you," I said. "Something important. A pair of eagles have been sighted not far from here. For a long time, eagles were considered an endangered species. They were dying out, and everyone was afraid they were going to disappear forever. But they haven't. Instead, their numbers are growing.

"Anyway, that's the reason I came by today. To tell you about the eagles. I remember what you once said to me. You said there are no eagles in this place at the edge of the earth. Well, they've come back, Jonah, and that means more will follow."

I looked up at the western sky, as if I expected to see an

eagle, its great wings outspread against the rose-gold of the setting sun. But the sky was clear, with only a few wispy evening clouds drifting across its pale surface.

But I *would* see an eagle someday. I knew I would. And it would look just like that—fine and beautiful and flying between the sun and the earth.

I touched his headstone gently in farewell and turned to go. "There will always be eagles, Jonah," I whispered. "They will never disappear. The brave and the strong will always survive."

In 2004, the National Museum of the American Indian will open its doors.

Situated in Washington, D.C., at the very foot of our nation's Capitol, the museum will contain more than 800,000 artifacts representing the history and culture of more than a thousand Native communities of the Western Hemisphere. It is estimated that six million people will visit the museum the first year alone.

The American Indians have survived near-annihilation. For many decades they had to struggle for their very existence. The injustices heaped upon them during those years cannot be forgotten. However, it is the future that is now the focus of their commitment—the safekeeping and perpetuation of their culture and identity as a people.

They will succeed. In the words of Jenny Muldoon, as she stood over Jonah Flying Cloud's grave, "The brave and the strong will always survive."

Author's Note

Every author has a book that is written from the heart. This is mine.

A few years ago, my husband, Duff, and I visited Carlisle Barracks, Pennsylvania, the second oldest army post in the United States. From 1879 to 1918 the Barracks was home to the Carlisle Indian School.

I knew very little about the history of the Indian boarding school system. All I knew was that for a number of years Indian children had been taken from their tribal communities and sent to schools similar to the one at Carlisle Barracks. I was only mildly interested to learn that the lovely guesthouse where we were staying had once been the school infirmary.

But then Duff and I went for a walk after dinner and discovered a small cemetery surrounded by a low fence. Stepping inside, we found ourselves among row upon row of white headstones, narrow and erect.

Buried beneath those headstones were Indian children with names like Louise Thunder, Cheyenne; Herbert J. Little Hawk, Sioux; Frances Bones, Comanche. The sad dates chiseled in the stones above them told me that many were not yet in their teens when they died.

Such young children, and so far from their homes and loved ones!

I lay awake all night thinking about those bleak little tombstones.

Surely, if any place, anywhere, deserves to be haunted, I thought, *it's here, the room where those children died, fright-*

ened and alone and without their families to give them comfort and courage.

In the novel I would later write, I had thirteen-year-old Jenny, whose bedroom had once been the Indian school infirmary and who has also visited the cemetery, spend a similarly sleepless night.

Throughout that long night I, like Jenny, kept expecting to see at my bedside the pale, anxious face of a young Indian ghost. No ghost appeared, yet I could almost sense a presence, a lingering miasma of sorrow.

When I returned home, a friend who is active in the Indian community told me the bitter story of those Indian boarding schools: how their stated purpose had been to make imitation white people out of "filthy savages," and how the children had been made to feel ashamed of who and what they were.

"There's a book here," I said. "You have to write it."

"No," she said. "*You* do."

So I did.

But first I had to do the research. It was a labor of love, for as I read the words of people who had miserably endured their years at Indian boarding schools, my fictional characters and the plot of the story began to come alive in my mind.

Jonah Flying Cloud is the composite of the many children whose reminiscences I read. His experiences at school are based on actual reported incidents: the use of force in the hair-cutting; the underfeeding; the beatings; the many deaths; the jailing of the disobedient and runaway students; the punishments for speaking a native language. The list goes on.

The story of Johnny Little Fox and his potato was inspired by an incident at one of the schools in the early years of the past century. The child's death was so heartbreaking that I knew I must write it into the story.

As for Swift Running River, his belligerent character was based on that of a young, real-life Indian student who, when he returned to his home in the Dakota territory, felt he was no longer considered an Indian by his people. Therefore, to prove his "Indianness," he shot and killed an army officer. At his trial he said, "I shot the lieutenant so I might make a place for myself among my people. Now I am one of them. I shall be hung and the Indians will bury me as a warrior. I am satisfied."

The Indian school Jonah attended is fictitious, but it is a mélange of many such schools across the country. Mr. Samuel, the superintendent of the school, is strictly the product of my imagination. There were the good and the bad, the kindly and the mean-spirited among those running the schools. I made Mr. Samuel one of the latter.

The facts that Jenny and Arnold stated in their history paper are true: How the white settlers' hunger for land as they moved ever westward contributed to what was called "the Indian Problem." And how, ultimately, Indian children were taken from their families and placed in government boarding schools in order to break them down, make them reject who they were, and then turn them into imitation white people.

Mrs. Swanson and her diary, however, are fictional, as are Fort Sayers and the town of Sayersville.

The *Kerria japonica* is a real rose. It was suggested to me by my writer friend, Brenda, who said it was the perfect flower for the story because of its strength and resilience. She also gave me a cutting, which I planted in my patio garden. It is now growing and spreading, just as Jenny's does on Swift Running River's grave.

I think of Jenny and Jonah every time I look at my *Kerria* rose. Once again I see them in my mind as I did when I wrote their story—the two of them meeting across time to find friendship and loving-kindness in the shadowland they called "the place at the edge of the earth."